SO GREAT A LOVE

T.M. CROMER

CHAPTER 1

$\mathcal{D}$eclan Braddock was only half-listening as Gavin Gardner, his business partner and best friend, droned on about the perfect getaway his wife had planned.

"So what do you think, D? Is it something you'd be interested in?"

The question brought him up short. He hoped his expression didn't give away that he had no idea what the hell the conversation had been about. He was afraid it did.

Gavin sighed in mock disgust. "You weren't listening."

"I'm sorry. I…" Really, there was no good excuse, and Declan couldn't get his head on straight. But ever since Claire left him, he'd been a distracted, surly asshat.

"No worries." Gavin took a chug of his beer and chased it with a handful of sketchy party mix from the dish on the bar.

As Declan waited for him to finish chewing, swallow, and repeat his long-winded dialogue, he grew impatient. The truth was, everything made him impatient and irritable these days. He was moody as fuck and couldn't seem to snap out of it. Yet if he were forced to be honest, his shitty attitude developed long before Claire walked out. His volatile temper had been the primary reason she'd called it quits. Or so she said. The situation was more complicated, and neither was left in doubt why.

Taking a sip of his virgin drink, he thought back to the day roughly five months ago when she'd pulled the plug on their seven-year marriage.

"I can't do this anymore, Declan. I won't," Claire said, tears streaming from her tragically haunted eyes.

He wanted to protest, to yell, to rage at fate, at her, at everything and everyone. Yet he feared if he started, he might never stop. So, with no outward emotion, he said, "Then go."

"That's your answer?" Her disbelief had left her slack-jawed with fists clenched at her sides. "Instead of fighting for our marriage, you tell me to go?"

"What do you want from me, Claire?" he finally exploded. "What? Tell me because I have no fucking idea what you expect from me."

"I expect you to be the old Declan I fell in love with! The man I married. I want him back."

Her anguished words had no impact.

"The old Declan is dead. I buried him with our son last January," he snarled.

He spun his chair and wheeled into the kitchen to get another drink. Booze was the only thing he found to numb the pain. Physical, mental, and worst, emotional.

The irony was not lost on him. It was a drunk driver who'd taken Jonah away from him, and now, Declan drank to forget.

· · ·

"Earth to Declan. Come in, Declan."

Shaking off the past, he cast Gavin a half smile. "Sorry. You were saying?"

"Bonnie thinks you should join us on our island vacation. What do you say?"

He arched a brow in question. "Gavin, do you realize how much of a pain in the ass it is for me to travel?"

"That's the beauty of it. We'll be going by private jet. No commercial airlines fly there."

"I don't know, man. Don't you and Bonnie want some private time? I'd feel like a third wheel. What the hell am I going to do on some island? Get my wheels stuck in the sand?" He sighed in the face of Gavin's unrelenting stare. "And should both of us be away from the office at the same time?"

"Okay, I'm going to answer your questions in reverse order. First, it's over the Thanksgiving holiday. The office would normally be closed, so we're just taking an extra day on either side of it. Second, you should take a break and enjoy a little fun in the sun. Have an island fling with one of the local hotties." When Declan rolled his eyes, Gavin gave him a light backhand against his shoulder. "Don't be a spoilsport. Let me live vicariously through your future sexual exploits. And third, Bonnie and I wouldn't have asked you if we didn't want you to go. We love you. So what about it?"

"I'm still not convinced we should both be out of town. Emergencies happen in the ad world all the time. One of us should be present to handle it."

"You know The Dragon can handle any emergency, plus some. She's nothing if not efficient. But if you tell her I admitted she could work circles around the two of us, I'll deny it to my dying day."

Declan chuckled but had to agree. Rachel, aka The Dragon Assistant, as Gavin preferred to call her, had been the best thing to happen to their firm. She'd started about eleven weeks ago and was already making a difference in their bottom line by bringing on new accounts. With her, their office ran like a well-oiled machine. Not to mention the steps she'd taken to coerce Declan into drying out by a stint in rehab.

"What are the exact dates? You know better than anyone that the holiday season is our most lucrative time of year. I don't need to tell you about Black Friday."

"And *you* know we already have all the ads created for the coming holidays. Any others Rachel can have signed off via the internet and digital proofs. It might surprise you to know that staff can work remotely in this day and age. Just say yes."

All of Declan's objections had been systematically removed, and because it was easier to give in, he agreed. With a whoop, Gavin ordered another round of drinks.

For Declan, it meant a whiskey sour punch sans the booze. Oddly enough, he didn't miss the alcohol. What he did miss was the numbing effect. Emotions rode too close to the surface these days.

A few hours later, Gavin adopted the excuse of pushing Declan's wheelchair to prop himself up, and the two of them made their way down the sidewalk to a waiting driver. As the cold fall air whipped around them and penetrated his thin jacket, he shivered. A tropical vacation might be the thing he needed most.

As they always did, his thoughts turned inward, and his wife wasn't far from the surface. Claire would've loved flying in a private jet to some remote island. Sober now, memories of her haunted him more and more. He'd heard from a mutual friend that she'd started to date again, and a knife to his heart would have hurt less. It wasn't lost on him that he'd effectively driven away the one person who made him feel complete.

But she deserved better.

A whole man. Not one who was broken in too many ways to count.

About a block away, Declan texted Bonnie to come outside and assist her husband into the house. She was waiting with a wry smile and another Uber.

"Hey, Bon Bon. I brought you a present," he said, gesturing to a staggering Gavin.

"Yeah, thanks. Just what I always wanted." Her dry tone had him chuckling.

"So, are you positive you want me tagging along on your vacation? Wouldn't you prefer some privacy?" He knew they'd been trying for a baby. He didn't imagine that his tagging along would allow them much alone time.

"You'll have a separate cabana at the resort. We'll get enough one-on-one time," she assured him.

"Okay, but won't Gavin mind if you spend all your nights with me?" he teased as he slid into the backseat.

"Oh, shut up!" Her laughter was the warmth he needed to ward off the chilly evening air. "For what it's worth, I'm glad you're going. I'll confirm the arrangements this week."

She closed the Uber door and went to round up her husband, who had stumbled off, singing at the top of his lungs.

The sight triggered another of Declan's rare grins. Those two were the only family he had left and the main thing that brought him even a smidgeon of joy. At the very least, a trip with them would be amusing. Gavin was always good for a laugh.

Declan glanced out over the aqua waters as they circled the small runway of Elysian Island. A private plane to an exclusive resort was definitely the best way to travel. He'd be spoiled forever and fully against any other transportation.

The scope of the place from this distance brought him a sense of peace. Why? He had no idea. Maybe this time away would help him get his life back on track. And maybe, after all he'd been through with the loss of his son and the pending divorce, he could salvage a modicum of normalcy. Perhaps he'd discover a way to come to terms with the past and plan for the future. Or that was his hope.

He snorted. Optimistic Declan rarely came out to play, but the idea of this particular vacation was weirdly uplifting.

The experts had said his back was healed, allowing him to walk, and they suggested his paralysis was merely psychological at this point. The new findings were bullshit, though. No one wanted to walk more than Declan. Hadn't he been killing himself with goddamned grueling physical therapy for almost two years? And despite regaining a minuscule amount of feeling in his legs, he still couldn't ditch the fucking chair.

God, how he wanted to. At night, his dreams consisted of walking, then running toward Claire and Jonah. But he could never quite reach them before cloying black smoke engulfed and obliterated them forever. When morning rolled around, he awoke drenched in sweat and, to his mortification, tears. If nothing else, this change of scenery would let him rest. Although he didn't have the nightmares every night, they were frequent enough to feed his chronic fatigue. And Declan was damned tired of being tired.

The landing was smooth and uneventful. The humiliating part was when Gavin and the pilot had to carry him down the steps where the resort vehicle waited. His condition was an ugly fact of life. The sooner he learned to live with the embarrassment of needing assistance, the easier it would become.

As if reading his thoughts, Gavin clasped a hand on his shoulder and said, "It's no big deal, D. I got my workout for the day."

"Speaking of workouts, they have a wonderful fitness center here with trained staff, and you can continue your PT sessions," Bonnie said brightly.

"Oh, joy!" Declan suppressed a sigh and pasted on a lopsided grin. "I thought I was on vacation?" he joked, trying to keep the conversation as light as them. He must've hit the right note because they both laughed.

"Let's go meet our hosts, shall we?" she asked after overseeing the loading of their luggage.

Twenty minutes later, they were ushered into the main lobby. The sheer splendor of the place sent Declan's jaw plunging. The opulence would make anyone glassy-eyed.

In the distance, the melodic thrumming of a steel drum filled the midday sky, and weirdly, he experienced a sense of coming home. As if, at this juncture in his life, he was where he needed to be.

"Have we died and gone to Heaven?" Gavin asked in hushed tones.

Bonnie laughed. "Didn't either of you read through the brochures I gave you?"

Declan and Gavin shared a sheepish glance.

"It's a good thing I know you both so well." With a shake of her head and a scolding tsk, she turned to greet a silver-haired goddess.

The woman graced Declan with a half smile as she approached. "Based on what I overheard, am I to assume Mrs. Gardner took it upon herself to complete in the fantasy requests for your stay? It's what we do here, fulfill our guests' innermost desires."

Her eyes were startling, boasting two different colors—one blue and the other a honey-brown. Her generous mouth widened further, displaying the perfect amount of white and giving the eerie impression that she saw straight into Declan's soul.

A shiver danced along his spine when she winked.

Winked!

What the hell did it mean?

Under her uncomfortable stare, he shifted and looked away, noticing her companion for the first time. He frowned at the Latino man who remained aloof but seemingly amused by their silent exchange. Declan received the impression they were a couple, and the guy indulged her every whim.

Their hostess's words finally sank in. He'd been so preoccupied by her multi-colored irises that he failed to register what she'd said.

"Wait. *Fantasy* requests?" Declan glanced between the resort owners. "Is this for real?"

"Yes. Each guest comes here seeking to play out a fantasy," the man replied. His rich voice was smooth, bordering hypnotic, and Declan shook his head, forcing himself to concentrate. "As Thalia said, here at Enchanted Tides Resort, we uncover and fulfill your deepest desires." The man paused a beat to let it sink in. "Allow me to make the introductions. I'm Alejandro Reyes. My lovely companion is Thalia De Wynter."

"Declan Braddock." He offered up a hand to shake. "I don't suppose anyone simply comes here to relax?" he asked, a sick feeling settling in the pit of his stomach.

"Not usually, no," his host confirmed.

"Great," he muttered, glaring at Bonnie.

He'd been set up. There was no telling what she'd signed him up for.

"Come, Mr. Braddock. We'll get a drink."

"I don't—"

"I know. For you, it will be a virgin rum punch. For me, a bourbon. I hope you don't mind," Alejandro interrupted smoothly.

Since Declan had no real choice, he followed. He got the distinct impression that this man's word was law on this island.

CHAPTER 2

Gavin and Bonnie had made themselves scarce when Declan returned from his little power talk with Alejandro. As well they should! They'd suckered him in with promises of rest and relaxation, but now, he was the victim of Bonnie's hare-brained scheme. Likely to introduce him to someone new. *Screw that!* He'd had his someone, and no other woman could compare to Claire.

A tall, willowy blonde on the other side of the courtyard caught his attention, and Declan's heart hammered harder than the steel drums. Were his thoughts so consumed with her that he imagined seeing her everywhere? The vision across the expanse of the pool presented her profile, and his lungs seized, failing to do their job.

Claire! She was really there!

Tan and happy with her long golden hair casually gathered in a high-riding ponytail, she glowed under the sun's afternoon light. Her pale pink halter dress, with its flowing skirt, danced with her long, lean legs as the breeze picked up.

Declan's ears zeroed in on her laughter, and all other sounds fell away. Though he was too far to see, he imagined her blue eyes were sparkling as she flirted with the tall blond man beside her. She lightly touched his chest, but it was Declan who felt it. How many times had she teased him in that exact same way? He was helpless to look away from so torturous a scene.

His heart spasmed, feeling squeezed by the tight fist of regret.

She must have sensed his stare, and she searched for the source. Horrified amazement flared in her wide eyes, and her hand flew to her mouth.

Christ!

He didn't care who he had to bribe, but he needed to get off this fucking island immediately. There was no way in hell he could bear witness to a weekend of her charming her new love interest. Alejandro mentioned there were a total of six additional couples over the holiday. With so few people in such an intimate setting, he was bound to see Claire and her boyfriend wherever he went.

Anger followed on the heels of Declan's hurt. Already vacationing with another man? Exploring "fantasies" with the guy? Yeah, she'd shucked her old life pretty fucking fast.

Declan tightened his grip on the wheels, surprised the pressure didn't pop the tubes. Gathering what little pride he had left, he nodded tightly and spun away. He had to find his cabin and hide like the wounded animal he was, at least until he could get off this godforsaken island.

The first person he spotted was Thalia. Standing to the far side of the pool deck, she observed him with a thoughtful expression on her face, almost troubled, as if seeing something dark and disturbing.

Yeah, well, he was feeling pretty goddamned dark at the moment!

With jerky motions, he steered himself to the nearest guest concierge. A quick check of her name tag revealed her name.

"Hey, Kim. I've had a bit of an emergency and need to head back to the States. When is the next flight off this island?"

She glanced over his head as if seeking silent permission. When she looked back at him, it was to convey regret. "I'm sorry, Mr. Braddock. Our flights run weekly. It's cost-prohibitive to fire up the jet unless absolutely necessary. Maybe we can be of assistance to you? What's the nature of your emergency, sir?"

He ignored her questions, desperate to escape. "What about a boat? Is anything heading into Panama? I can catch a commercial flight from there."

"No, sir. Again, they only run once a week."

"Look, Kim—"

"Declan?" Claire's tentative address gutted him.

He closed his eyes. Agast to discover moisture building, he fisted his hands against his closed lids and willed the tears back.

Fuck.

He was five seconds from breaking down and sobbing like an infant in front of all these happy-go-lucky tourists. Ignoring Claire, he violently rolled toward the lobby. From there, he was sure to remember the direction of his cabana, right? His wordless, abrupt departure was unforgivably rude, but Claire should be used to his atrocious behavior by now.

. . .

Claire gaped at Declan's retreating back.

Two minutes ago, she was convinced she was imagining things. There he'd sat, looking like she'd taken a club to his head. Before she could react, he was off in the opposite direction. She'd shoved her drink in the hands of the nearest waiter and run around the deck to get to Declan.

But once again, she felt like a damn fool when he failed to acknowledge her. Too many times in the almost two years since Jonah died, Declan had chosen to purposely ignore her, whizzing away in his fucking wheelchair as if she didn't exist. As time progressed, he'd become worse, refusing to do anything to make life easier. She should be used to his atrocious behaviors, which, along with his drunken rages, had forced her to leave.

But she wasn't and never would be.

"I'm sorry," Claire said to Kim. "Declan is..."

What? How did she explain the greatest man she'd ever known was now a raging asshole?

To see him here, in this setting, completely discombobulated her. She was supposed to meet her best friends for a week of R&R. It never occurred to her that Bonnie and Gavin would drag Declan along, or that they could. Her soon-to-be ex was notoriously difficult to separate from either the bottle or his beloved work.

Somewhere along the way, Claire had heard he entered rehab and was finally participating in the prescribed physical therapy. She'd wept at the news. Filled with hope, she had expected Declan to call, giving them a chance to truly talk things through, or perhaps reconcile.

Every day, she waited for the phone to ring, and each evening, she was distraught when it didn't.

He'd never contacted her. Not once since she walked out.

Feeling hopeless and looking for a distraction, she'd finally said yes to a client who had been pressing for a date.

Of course, her dinner with Martin had been a disaster from the start. Why she said yes to a second and third was beyond her comprehension. Maybe it was because she'd been so lost and lonely. He'd been a bit geeky but nice enough, and after their fourth outing, she'd slept with him, hoping to chase away the ghosts of her past.

Claire cringed whenever she thought about the experience. Terrible didn't begin to describe it. His loud, lusty grunts and premature ejaculation had embarrassed them both. Then, he dressed in a hurry, berating *her* the entire time and saying things like if she hadn't been so frigid, she'd have come. After an hour-long shower in which she'd scrubbed herself raw, she wrote off that chapter of her life as a major mistake. Swearing only to move forward and to stop looking back or playing the "what if" game, she did just that. There were some days harder than others, but she concentrated on getting through, on becoming stronger with each passing hour.

Loneliness didn't have a place in her life.

"Enough is enough," she said. It had become her mantra. And yes, she was talking to herself, but who cared at this point?

Across the distance, she caught Thomas's eye and smiled her apology.

They'd met at the local coffeehouse, and the charming Thomas Sullivan had turned out to be sweet, gorgeous, and a whole lot of fun. Coincidentally, they were both in the process of getting divorced and had much in common.

After four and a half weeks of dating, she'd been approached by Bonnie about this trip. In a moment of madness, she'd asked Thomas to join her, thinking it would be a good time to consummate their new relationship and possibly get to know him better.

Now here she stood, feeling crushed after the love of her life wheeled off into the sunset without her. Her guilt at leaving Thomas to fend for himself was building, and she imagined her defection went over harder than a lead balloon. The urge to run and hide was overwhelming. Her desire to cry even more so, and she shifted to hide her reaction from him. If her spastic behavior didn't chase him away, certainly a meltdown in the middle of paradise would.

At the first opportunity, she intended to kill Bonnie and bury her body neck deep in the sand.

Light footsteps and a scraping of a lounge chair sounded from behind, right before a hard, muscled arm encircled her waist. Thomas drew her back against him and kissed the crown of her head.

She squirmed within his embrace, and it was all she could do not to pull away. How he held her was too eerily similar to Declan whenever he'd tried to comfort her after a trying day.

But mainly, her skin felt too tight for her body, like it might split open and spill her bones onto the travertine pavers at his feet, and she wanted Thomas to stop touching her. Unreasonable, she knew, but still, the desire to flee was awful and pressing.

"You okay, babe?"

She nodded, not trusting herself to speak.

"The ex?"

Again, she dipped her head to indicate the affirmative,

still staring at the space where Declan had been. She'd confided in him after a night of wining and dining followed by enough tears to turn a man off forever. But he'd been understanding, calling on her the following morning with a hangover cure.

Thomas was as sweet as the day was long.

"Want to go back to our cabin and talk?" he asked gently.

Claire shook her head. The last thing she cared to do was discuss Declan. If she opened the floodgate, she'd drown them both this go around.

"I need to find Bonnie and discover why this happened. Why don't I meet you back here in about an hour or so?" she asked.

"Sure. I should unpack the rest of my things and press my suit before dinner anyway."

"Thanks."

As he moved to kiss her, she presented her cheek. It hadn't been intentional, and his baffled look hurt her stomach. There wasn't a plausible excuse for her behavior, so she remained mute.

When she shifted away, another hand touched her waist.

"Why the hell is everyone so grabby today?" she snapped, assuming it was Bonnie and preparing to rip her a new one.

But Claire was brought up short at seeing Thalia wearing a soft, understanding expression.

"Mrs. Braddock, I'd like a few minutes of your time, if possible."

"Call me Claire." After all, the surname Braddock wouldn't be hers much longer. The sooner she got used to it, the better.

"Of course. *Claire*."

They strolled through the foyer until they overlooked the luminescent turquoise waters surrounding the island.

Minutes dragged without her hostess reaching the point, and Claire broke the uncomfortable silence.

"What did you wish to discuss?"

"Your husband."

Huh! She hadn't seen that one coming!

"Declan?"

"Yes, he's not a very happy man, Claire. I think you and I can do something about it."

"Begging your pardon, Thalia, but I don't see where it's my problem or your business," she replied coolly. "Declan has taken every opportunity to reject me, as he did again tonight. Right now, I just want to enjoy my vacation. What that asshole does is his own business."

Okay, maybe she regurgitated a little TMI and expressed too much of her simmering rage, but what the fuck? What gave this stranger the right to delve into her relationship?

"But you still love him, no?" There was no real question behind Thalia's comment, and the statement was powerful in its simplicity.

Claire snorted her disbelief at the woman's audacity. Yet, as she stared into those understanding, mismatched eyes, her anger melted away, and her tragic story poured out.

"It was New Year's Eve. It wasn't that late, maybe nine o'clock or so. Because I'd only had half a glass of wine and Declan had overindulged, we determined it was better if I drove home." Pausing for a cleansing breath, she smiled bitterly. "We also decided to pick up our son from my mother's instead of waiting until morning. He'd had a slight fever earlier in the day, and I felt like the worst parent for leaving him. I needed to make sure he was okay. Plus, we figured any serious partiers weren't on the roads yet."

"You were wrong about the last bit," Thalia stated matter-of-factly.

Claire nodded, feeling cold to her soul. "A drunk driver ran the stop sign. We were only a mile from home. Can you believe it?"

Though she asked the question, she didn't expect a response. In the months after, she'd read that most accidents happened within five miles of a person's residence. Theirs was just one more fucking statistic.

"What happened then?" Thalia asked softly.

"The bastard T'd us on the passenger side. Declan and Jonah took the brunt of it. Our son was killed instantly, and Declan, well, you can see he was paralyzed from the waist down."

"Your marriage fell apart with the loss of your child." Again, a matter-of-fact statement and not a question.

"Yes," Claire confirmed, though she didn't need to. Her retelling became choppy as she fought against the crushing guilt and pain. "Declan began to drink. Hard liquor. Day and night. He was trashed constantly. Every day worse than the last. He was hurting, and I didn't know how to help him."

A wine glass was thrust in her hand, and she sipped the refreshing liquid, recalling the past. "He refused to go to work. Refused to seek psychological help. Or any professional help at all, really. His constant refusal to follow the doctor's orders regarding physical therapy was a major bone of contention between us."

"Yet, you hung on for quite a long while."

"Not long enough. But after seventeen months of hell, I

had to get out. I'd made one last-ditch effort to get him to return to his former self—to return to me—but he wouldn't. He didn't want to. The warm, caring man I married was gone. In his place was an unfeeling bastard." She gulped more wine. "It was as if his soul died in place of Jonah's."

"And you?"

"Me what?"

"How did you cope with the loss of your family?"

"Therapy. In the beginning, I went twice a week because I couldn't get through a day without sobbing. Time helped." Claire sighed and faced Thalia. "First, I got through one twenty-four-hour period, then another. Pretty soon, I managed to get through an entire week without breaking down. When I left Declan, I started the bi-weekly appointments again. After the first month, I was stronger, and they tapered off."

"You've had a rough couple of years, haven't you?" Thalia murmured, stroking her shoulder. The action was bizarrely comforting.

And there was little need to answer, but she did anyway. "Labeling it as rough is one hell of an understatement."

CHAPTER 3

A pounding sounded on the door of his cabin, and Declan checked his watch.

Seven-fifteen.

Some days he fucking hated Gavin's prompt nature.

"Come in!" he hollered over his shoulder, continuing to struggle with his damned tie. Claire had always helped him in the past, taking over when he declared himself all thumbs. "Are these damned things optional? Because I'm about to shove it down the trash compactor."

"You don't have a trash compactor," Gavin said with a grin.

"Whatever."

"And no, they're not necessary. I'm not wearing one either."

Declan sighed his relief, balled the material, and flung it across the room, or as far as a tie could be thrown.

"Have a care, man. That's the one Bonnie gave you for your birthday. It's silk."

He rolled his eyes.

Gavin was born finicky about clothing. Honestly, Declan had been just as picky before the accident. But with all the food spills, falls in transitioning, and dirt from his tires, he'd gotten away from spending a fortune on his wardrobe. The whopping support check for Claire each month also put a kink in his purchasing habits. She never asked for the money, but after what he'd put her through, it was the least he could do.

Claire.

Likely, he'd see her in the dining room.

In the past few hours, he'd come to grips with the reality of her presence on the island. Surely he could turn off the caring center of his brain, right? He'd managed it daily since being served the divorce papers. But his heart? Yeah, that was another matter.

He prayed for the strength to be civil.

"Ready?" Gavin asked, coming up behind the chair.

"Yeah."

They walked in silence down the long corridor, but Declan needed answers.

"Did you know Claire was vacationing here, too?"

"No."

He put his hands on the wheels to stop their progress and twisted in his chair. If he could see Gavin's expression, look him in the eyes, he might discern the truth for himself.

"Really?"

His friend's hazel gaze was direct. "I swear, Declan, I didn't know. I found out late this afternoon after you left with Alejandro. Bonnie knows damned well I would never be party to setting you up for heartache."

Declan nodded. "Thanks, man."

The tension between them abated, and they continued the journey to the dining room.

"At least she'll be sitting at another table," he muttered.

"Uh, D, about that…" Gavin trailed off into uncomfortable silence.

As if by some strange coincidence, the path between them and the table cleared as couples found their seats. The lights in the overhead chandeliers seemed to flare brighter as they highlighted the woman across from Bonnie. And sitting proudly beside Claire was her devastatingly handsome companion.

"Fuck!"

"De—"

"Look, do me a solid and tell everyone I'm sick." He sure as shit would be if he had to endure a meal with his soon-to-be-ex wife and that fucktwat boyfriend of hers.

"Too late. We've been spotted."

Declan swore.

Claire was a vision in her gold, sequined dress, and she stole Declan's breath. When she rose to welcome them, something stirred to life within him, and he rubbed the spot over his heart.

Love.

The one emotion he thought would lie forever dormant.

"Declan."

Her voice was smooth, polite—as was her visage. Not a trace of her feelings reflected.

When had she become the more stoic of the two of them? His Claire-bear's emotions were always close to the surface, ready to bubble over at any moment. And he fucking hated her cool, reserved mask. She didn't do reserved.

"Claire," he returned gruffly. It was his best attempt at being nice, but not so easy when he really wanted to smash all the china in the room. "How are you?"

A flicker.

He might've imagined it in her eyes. Those cornflower blue, expressive orbs. He knew the exact color because he'd looked it up the day they'd met. Funny how those odd things were hitting him tonight. Still, that flicker made him believe she wasn't as serene as she appeared.

"I'm good." She didn't ask after him, which was surprising. Usually, she was the first one to put someone at ease and ask how they were.

A throat cleared. It could have been Gavin or possibly Claire's date. The awkwardness of the situation didn't escape anyone at the table. Yet, he found it damned near impossible to tear his gaze from hers.

Softly, too softly for anyone to hear, he said, "I'm glad."

But *she* heard. She who was always so attuned to him, as he'd been attuned to her. With no conscious thought other than to touch her, he clasped her hand and entwined their fingers like he'd always done and brought her hand to his mouth. He dropped a light kiss on her palm, then released her.

A sheen of tears, hers or his, he couldn't tell, came down like a curtain between them. Most likely his since the rest of the table was a blur. He blinked rapidly, noticing she did the same.

His heart pinged as she pasted on an overbright smile and said, "I'm starved. What's everyone having?"

She'd played at being cheerful a lot in the days after Jonah died. Strictly for the outside world's benefit because Declan had been such an ass to her. Yet each time, she'd put on her patently false smile and ignore his horrific behavior. It had gotten to the point he'd become spiteful, doing things to see if he could break her.

She never broke.

Not once.

And he'd resented her for being the strong one. The truth was hard to bear, but he now recognized it for what it was. He'd once believed it was because she'd left him, but the truth was that his bitterness resulted from the death of their son and the broken back. Neither had destroyed her as they had him.

Lost in his memories, he missed the conversational thread. The silent stares penetrated his subconscious.

"I'm sorry. Woolgathering." He offered up a wry smile.

"We were discussing dinner options." Bonnie tapped his menu, and he obliged by selecting a main course.

The waiter came and left, and Declan couldn't recall what he'd ordered. It mattered not at all because the food tasted like sawdust in his dry mouth. He continued to chew so he wouldn't have to join the conversation.

Under the influence of the rich, flavorful wine, Gavin recounted humorous stories from their earlier life. No one surpassed his ability to tell a tale. Anyone within hearing distance leaned in to listen and chuckled at the best parts. Then, he described the day Declan met Claire, and as the story progressed, a hush fell over the room.

Like a tractor beam, Declan's gaze was drawn to Claire's beloved face. Her attention was focused on Gavin, and tears shimmered in her large eyes. One hand held her wine suspended halfway to her lips, as if she'd forgotten her intent to sip it, her other rested at the base of her throat.

"...And after he dropped her off that night, he swore to anyone who would listen that he planned on making her his wife. It took him what? Eight months?" Gavin looked at Bonnie for confirmation.

"Seven months, nineteen days, and twenty-two hours," Declan supplied, still hypnotized by the raw emotion Claire unknowingly displayed.

Several women around them sighed as if his response were the most romantic they'd heard.

"Uh, right, a little over seven months to convince her to say yes. I'd never seen a happier man before or since," Gavin finished and raised his glass. "To Declan and Claire."

"To Declan and Claire!" the crowd chorused.

A blush spread across her pale complexion. She darted a quick glance first at him and then at Thomas, who was sitting to her right, desperately trying to suppress his ire—and failing.

Had Gavin purposely tried to get under the other man's skin? If so, Declan would buy him a drink at their first opportunity.

The crowd dispersed after dinner, off to find entertainment on their first night of vacation. Gavin and Bonnie offered to spend time with Declan, but it didn't take a genius to guess they wanted to be alone. Their not-so-subtle glances and soft smiles spoke of their need for privacy.

Declan waved them away, then wheeled out to the pool deck to watch couples pair off and sway to the soft island music.

"Declan."

Claire.

He hung his head, knowing he couldn't avoid this confrontation forever. Suppressing his desire to make a run for it, he sighed and spun to face her.

And he thanked Christ she was alone!

Had the handsome Thomas been with her, he might have thrown up on the guy's polished leather shoes.

"Can we talk?" she asked tentatively. A shiver accompanied her words.

He shrugged out of his suit jacket and passed it to her. "Of course."

She slipped it on and perched on the closest lounger.

"I didn't know you'd be here. I would never be so crass as to bring... well, I wouldn't—couldn't—do that to you."

She meant to be kind, but Declan felt the sting, all the same. Pity was intermingled within her jumbled words, and it scraped his nerves raw. Still, he was determined to be a better person than he had been. She deserved to be happy, even if he suffered at seeing her start a new life with someone else.

"It's alright, sweet—." He cleared his throat. The old endearment snuck up on him. "I..." He heaved a frustrated sigh and focused on her tightly clasped hands, with knuckles showing white.

A bitter smile curled his lips.

Claire despised confrontation. And she was already anticipating his explosion. Shame swamped him. His past behavior had conditioned her, making her gun-shy around him.

He covered her hands and entwined their fingers a second time. Her surprised gaze studied him, and her fearful hesitation caused him to avoid her probing stare. Ever so gently, he traced the delicate veins on the back of her other hand. Her bones seemed so fragile compared to his. Yet she was the strong one—she always had been.

They sat for the longest while, neither willing to break the contact. Declan recalled the first time she'd touched him. She'd run the pads of her fingertips over the sharp planes of his face, caressing his jaw, smoothing the confused frown between his brows, dipping her index finger between his lips. The suggestive invitation had needed no words, and he'd pounced on her like a man starved.

Yes, he remembered the night well. They'd made love until dawn, calling in sick the next morning because they were loath to leave the warmth of their nest. They seemed so young then. He'd been twenty-six and she, twenty-four. Full of hope. Five months later, they'd moved in together, and two months afterward, they'd become engaged. A year and a half after that, they'd married.

Yet here they were, roughly ten years later, separated, with many good and bad memories between them. The bitterest being Jonah's senseless death. Declan remembered a grief counselor spouting some stupid statistic about marriages not surviving the loss of a child. He'd be damned if he could recall the number. But he fucking hated that they'd become part of the failed-relationship percentage. He'd have sworn nothing could ever keep them apart.

"So, are you serious about this guy?" Oh, for fuck's sake! Where the hell had that bullshit come from? He barely refrained from punching himself in the fucking face.

"I don't know. I like him. He's kind," she answered, voice hardly above a whisper.

Still, Declan winced at the word "kind." He sure as shit

hadn't been. No, he'd been rude and hurtful—spiteful at every turn.

"Kind is good," he said, meaning it.

"Are you? Seeing anyone special?"

A harsh laugh escaped him. Did she really need to ask and make him appear all the more pathetic? Finally, he met her searching eyes and allowed her to see the honesty and the residual love he felt for her.

"No, Claire. There's no one. Can you imagine anyone signing on for all of this?" He swept a hand down his body and meant to make it lighthearted. In reality, it sounded a lot like self-pity and loathing.

"Don't do that, Declan. Don't make jokes at your own expense. No one finds it funny." Fury was underlying her words.

Feeling foolish and set adrift, he dropped her hand.

"What did you expect? You want me to say I'm happy you found someone? That you were able to forget what we shared for ten years? I won't do that, sweetheart. I'm not that big of a person. Not when I'm still here, still in lo—" He shook his head in frustration. "I guess I'm not as ready for this conversation as I thought. Goodnight, Claire."

He whipped around to go.

"Declan!"

The crack in her voice brought him up short. What either of them would have said was lost as another couple knocked into his chair, sending him careening toward the deep end of the pool. He grabbed for the wheels, but the momentum was too great, and his tire caught on the edge. For him, the incident happened in slow motion, though it took mere seconds.

Just as the water closed over his head, Claire's scream

rang out. The weight of the chair, coupled with the water, pinned him to the bottom. As he struggled to dislodge it and the last of his air left his lungs, he had a ridiculous desire to laugh.

Some fucking drunk was going to take him out one way or another. Perhaps he should accept his fate.

CHAPTER 4

Wen Claire witnessed Declan pitch into the pool, she screamed and dove after him. The muted splashes of additional swimmers followed closely behind hers. Obviously, she hadn't thought this through, or she'd have kicked off her heels and shed the evening gown now absorbing water at an alarming rate. The weight dragged her down, and she fumbled with the zipper, managing to untangle her limbs from the clinging fabric. Left only in her lacy bra and panties, she swam toward Declan.

He twisted uselessly back and forth, his chest pressed to the bottom of the pool, and bubbles bursting from his soundless shout rose all around them.

She reached him right as two resort staffers arrived. Working in tandem, they eased the chair back, allowing Claire access to Declan. She grabbed for him and pushed off the pool's bottom for all she was worth. Although their heads broke the surface simultaneously, Declan wasn't a lightweight by any stretch, and she struggled to keep them afloat. The water made him slightly more buoyant, but his soaked clothing worked to drag them back down.

Claire shifted their position to hold his head above water and sidestroked toward the shallow end of the over-sized pool. Luckily, he was smart enough not to fight her and, using his arms, helped propel them faster. When she thought she couldn't lift her shoulder for another stroke, two men arrived to relieve her of her burden. She dragged herself to the steps, collapsing half in and half out of the water.

A subtle movement at the far end of the pool caught her attention. Her gold, sequined dress was wrapped around the wheelchair in a tight embrace. It felt like a sign she shouldn't have given up on her marriage so soon, but she shook it off. Staying for one more minute in a toxic situation would've been foolish to the extreme. If Declan didn't murder her, she certainly would've killed him.

He rested beside her, shooed away the resort employees hovering around him, and gestured toward the submerged chair.

"I'll need my wheelchair, if you would be so kind, fellas."

The entire fiasco was so freaking ridiculous that she giggled. Declan's disbelief had her laughing harder. After a shocked pause, he chuckled right along with her. Once their hilarity died, he snaked an arm around her shoulders and dropped a featherlight kiss on her temple.

"You saved my life, Claire-bear. In some cultures, it means you're now responsible for me."

She snorted and half-heartedly shoved him. "Right."

"What? You don't like these midnight swims?" he teased.

Another giggle escaped, and she gave in to temptation, snuggling into his embrace. How long had it been since he had held her? It seemed like an eternity.

"I don't think I'd mind so much if you'd outfit your chair with automatic inflatable flotation devices."

"A James Bond chair? Hm, not a bad idea." His fingers tightened. "You design the prototype, and I'll market the hell out of them. We'll be millionaires in no time."

"Deal."

She shivered in the cool night air and shifted closer to his warmth. His fingers brushed the underside of her breast, creating a tingling awareness. She enjoyed the sensation, but god, she was pitiful. Why was she clinging to any hint of Declan's affection, getting turned on by an innocent touch?

"Um, sweetheart?"

When she glanced up, she was caught by his warm regard. As his hot gaze dipped below her neckline, her nipples hardened under the wet lace.

His darkening eyes returned to her face, making it only as far as her lips. The desire in his hot gaze was difficult to ignore, and when he dipped his head toward her, Claire met him halfway. The kiss was soft, sweet in its simplicity. It also turned her on so badly that she wanted to crawl into his lap. Wanted to straddle him, wrap her legs around his lean hips, and press her core to his. Her relentless need to get lost in the touch she craved bordered on pathetic.

Close by, a throat cleared, making the person's discomfort evident. Yet, they were reluctant to part. She didn't know who became aware of their audience first. Probably Declan.

Alejandro Reyes sounded amused as he produced a towel. "Mrs. Braddock, allow me to assist you."

"Shoot me now," she muttered and buried her flaming face against Declan's shoulder. A snarfing laugh escaped him. Drawing back, she hit him with the full force of her glare. "Why do you always get me into these compromising situations and then laugh at my embarrassment?"

A grin practically split his face. "I don't know. Maybe it's so fun to tease you."

There he was—her old Declan. Pain and joy stabbed her heart. Oh, god, how she'd missed him!

"Mrs. Braddock," Alejandro prompted.

Still staring at her love's handsome features, she rose and wrapped the towel around her. Declan's deep sigh of regret made her heart sing.

"It's a crime against humanity for you to cover all that gorgeousness," he murmured, capturing her attention.

But she was certain she imagined it, and when she looked back down, his attention was focused on someone across the deck.

Following his line of vision, she saw Thomas and gulped.

He was seething.

A glance at Declan showed his very self-satisfied look, and unease unfurled in her belly. Surely he didn't intend to sabotage her vacation? She asked herself if she minded and realized she didn't. The incident and her reaction brought her shame to the surface and propelled her the rest of the way out of the water.

No way in hell was she about to set herself up for heartache again. Been there, done that. And she should buy the damned T-shirt as a reminder.

Part of her expected Thomas to storm off or at least blow up about the kiss he'd witnessed. But the solicitous behavior he showed was baffling. And when he placed one arm around her shoulders to lead her back to their cabana, Claire couldn't help but look back one last time.

Declan remained, ignoring the offers of help, hyper-focused on their retreating forms. The intensity of his stare could be felt along every inch of her exposed skin. Across the distance, he met her fretful stare. The bastard had the audacity to wink. Preventing a responding smile was impossible. The man still held her heart, and there wasn't anything about him that didn't appeal to her on every level.

With a deep sigh, she allowed herself to be led away.

Watching another man walk away with his wife went against every fiber of Declan's being. The near drowning clarified one thing—he wanted Claire back and would do whatever it took to get her. The pumped-up playboy didn't deserve a woman as incredible as his Claire-bear.

The smile she'd cast Declan went a long way toward soothing his battered soul. She wasn't indifferent to him. He could work with that. All that was left to do was prove he was a changed man and had no intention of breaking her heart again—if she'd only let him back in.

"Declan?"

He jerked his gaze away from Claire's retreating back, surprised Gavin wasn't with Bonnie. "Hey, man. I thought you were working on baby-making."

Gavin snorted. "We argued about her underhanded matchmaking and how it backfired."

While Declan appreciated his friend going to bat for him, he felt terrible that he might have been the cause of a rift between them. "You didn't need to do that, Gav. I'm a big boy."

With a snort, Gavin entered the pool. "Let's get you out and dried off."

Back in his room, Declan poured him a scotch and grabbed a water for himself. He lifted his plastic bottle in a toast. "To Bonnie and Claire."

"To Bonnie and Claire." Gavin raised his glass and then took a sip. "Do you suppose they know how much they drive us crazy?"

Declan barked a laugh. His second one of the night—imagine that! It was as if seeing Claire tonight had popped the cork of his emotional blockage. Smiling wasn't a chore. Laughter became real, unforced. "Isn't that every female's job?"

"Probably in their handbook somewhere."

A long moment passed before Gavin addressed the issue at hand. "So. Claire."

"Yeah."

"She's looking great, huh?"

Declan cast his well-meaning buddy a wry glance.

"I wonder what she sees in that clown."

"Stability?" Declan suggested. "A guy who sees the diamond she is and doesn't treat her like garbage?"

"Come on, D. You never did that."

"I did. After Jona—well, after, they forced me to come to grips with it in rehab. To acknowledge my behavior." Declan took a long swallow of water, wishing for something much stronger. Voice cracked and raw, he said, "I want her back, Gavin. More than I've wanted just about anything else in my entire life, I want her back."

"Okay. Then we'll come up with a plan."

His friend's support humbled him. No judgment. No doubt whatsoever that Declan could achieve his goal.

Finding the words to express his thanks was impossible. Instead, he cleared his throat and blinked away tears. Christ, he was such a fucking mess.

"The only thing I've come up with so far is to throw Tommy Boy off a cliff," he confessed. "It's going to be difficult in this thing, though."

"Not with two of us."

"I love that you always have my back, man. You know I don't deserve it," Declan said, suddenly serious. "I haven't always been the greatest of friends to you."

"We've been best friends since we were six, D. You've always been there for me. Remember how you used to hide me when my old man would knock the shit out of me? Yeah, dealing with a few months of your drunk ass was a walk in the park by comparison." Gavin clasped his shoulder. "Besides, you had good reason. We all got that. Even Claire. She left because she didn't know how to help you and couldn't stand to see you drinking yourself into an early grave."

Uncomfortable with this particular line of conversation, Declan changed the subject. "They say nothing's keeping me from walking."

"What?"

"My last appointment. The doctor said nothing is keeping me in this chair. They believe it's possible, at this point, that my inability to walk is psychological. Maybe a manifestation of guilt because I lived and Jonah didn't."

Gavin dropped into the nearest chair, and his shell-shocked expression resembled how Declan had felt hearing the same thing from Dr. Felder. It was difficult to conceive that anyone would remain in a wheelchair if they didn't have to. But his paralysis didn't *feel* like it was in his head. Yes, he had sensation in his legs now, maybe not as much as before the accident, but certainly not enough to walk or hold himself up. The physical therapy appointments were grueling, and while he did experience the pain that went along with exercise, the motion of standing and putting one leg in front of the other seemed next to impossible. However, his medical team refused to give up, insisting it was time for Declan to get on board and want it bad enough to achieve the goals they'd set.

"Tomorrow morning, I see the medical staff they've set up for me here. Alejandro mentioned acupuncture and meditation during our meet and greet. Said Thalia feels it's necessary to clear out some chakras or some hokey bullshit. Sounds pretty new age, but at this point, I won't reject anything."

"The woman frightens me. It's her eyes. Like they see everything."

He got exactly what Gavin was saying. She need only cast one long look in his direction, and all his body hair stood on end. In the past, she'd have been burned as a witch, without a doubt.

Unsure why he needed to defend her, Declan said, "Oddly enough, I think she has everyone's best interests at heart."

Any further discussion was cut off by a knock on the door.

"You expecting anyone?" Gavin asked on his way to answer it.

Declan snorted his amusement. "Yeah, my girlfriend," he snarked.

Gavin's grin flashed as he whipped open the door.

Neither of them expected Claire to be standing there, suitcase in hand. Mouths open, they stared.

"I wondered... I mean..." She cleared her throat and tried again. "Do you mind if I stay here tonight?"

CHAPTER 5

Taking in the stunned expression on both men's countenances, Claire worried she'd miscalculated by coming here. Perhaps she should have checked with the reception desk if there were any spare rooms.

Gavin was the first to recover and ushered her into the room.

"Claire, what are you doing here? Is everything okay?" Declan asked.

The genuine concern in his voice as he wheeled toward her nearly brought her to tears. *This* was the man she loved within minutes of meeting. He had to hate that she was here with Thomas, but he hadn't been mean or nasty. His deepest desire was for her to be happy and provide whatever he could to make it happen.

She glanced at Gavin in a silent plea for him to go so she could speak privately with Declan. Thankfully, he picked up the cue and made his excuses. His leaving allowed them some much-needed alone time, and it was imperative they clear the air.

Yet when she looked into Declan's concerned, expectant face, the words wouldn't come.

He shifted closer, clasping her clammy palm in his. If it were possible, his tone gentled more, as if he were talking to a frightened child. "Claire-bear, talk to me. Did he hurt you?"

And because Thomas hadn't, because he was actually a decent guy, she spoke the truth. "No, Declan. It's nothing like that."

He removed the suitcase from her death-grip and reached for her other hand. With no choice, she allowed him to tug her forward to settle into his lap. The sensation was odd. When they were younger and she'd had a rough day, she curled up on his lap to tell him about her woes. She'd desperately missed their closeness since the loss of Jonah. Declan wouldn't have dreamed of holding her like this while he was in his "damned contraption" only a mere few months ago.

Yet, here she sat, reveling in the feeling of being close to him again. While his thighs weren't as muscled as they'd been, they were still strong and toned beneath her. And if he wasn't as fit below the waist as he'd once been, his upper body certainly made up for it. His arms were like steel bands as they wrapped around her and hugged her close. The rock-hard chest made her mouth water, and she longed to feel under his form-fitting t-shirt to explore all his delicious ridges.

He smelled the same, too. Clean, addictive, and pure Declan. Without meaning to, she nuzzled his neck and brushed her lips against his throat. She trailed light kisses along his jaw, not minding the roughness of his day-old stubble.

"Not that I don't appreciate the hell out of what you're doing, sweetheart, but can you tell me what's going on?"

His voice was rough and aroused. Had she not known from experience, the solid ridge of his penis against her hip would have told her all she needed to know.

She debated how much she wanted to confess and decided to go for broke. "I came on vacation believing I might finally move on. I planned to sleep with Thomas and take our relationship to the next level." She inhaled deeply before gushing, "I couldn't do it, Declan. After seeing you today, after having had your arm around me in the pool, I realized I wasn't ready for another man to touch me again."

His heart raced beneath her palm, and he waited an inordinately long minute before he spoke. "What are you saying, Claire? You don't want to date Thomas?"

"I don't know. I only know I couldn't be with him tonight. Not after seeing you again. But staying in our cabin and forcing him to sleep on the couch was wrong."

His heart slowed to a dull thud. "I see."

What did he see? What had he read into her words? She wanted to ask, but his past rejections haunted her, seizing her vocal cords.

His lips brushed her temple, and he helped her to stand. As he positioned himself to wheel away, his knuckles whitened on top of the tires.

Feeling like a fool for assuming he'd want her, she grabbed her bag's handle and avoided eye contact. "I can see if they have another c-cabin."

"Don't be ridiculous. You'll stay here. Take the bed."

"No. I—"

"It's late, Claire," he said gently.

"Okay, but I'll take the couch. I'm not chasing you out of your bed, Declan."

"You're not. I'm up and down a lot during the night anyway. It's easier to transition from the couch since it's the same height as my chair."

"But—"

He held up a hand to cut her off. "Please stop. It's not up for debate. I may have lost the use of my legs, but I damned well haven't lost my manners."

"What size bed is it? Why can't we share?"

His sharp inhale indicated his surprise. "If we share, I won't be able to keep my hands off you, Claire," he said roughly.

The thrill of excitement zipped along her nerve endings. She told herself she was a sucker for punishment, but she had absolutely no problem with sex if he wanted it. Hell, she welcomed it.

"If you're worried, we can put a friendship pillow between us on the bed," she suggested.

What the hell made her say that? Now he'd think she didn't want him.

Smile sardonic, he waved a hand, gesturing toward the bedroom. "After you, sweetheart."

As Claire stepped around Declan, the subtle scent of her perfume teased his senses. Years ago, when they'd honeymooned in Paris, they came across a small perfumery. There, a woman concocted unique batches based on the customer's body chemistry. When mixed with the skin, the fragrance elicits an intoxicating aroma. The one Declan had purchased for Claire was one he'd never tire of. Each year, for their anniversary, he had gifted her with a brand new bottle.

Except for this most recent one.

Yes, he'd acquired more, but the gift-wrapped package remained at the top of his bedroom closet. He'd considered forwarding it to her, but eventually decided against it. If he dared to approach her, she'd likely dump the fucking thing over his stupid head.

Caught up in the memories and watching her perfect ass encased in those beautiful, skimpy shorts, he failed to register she'd stopped walking. As she waited for him in the entry to the bedroom with a soft smile, his heart began to hammer painfully. Her look was reminiscent of better times when they were happy.

Blood surged into his dick, giving him his second stiffy of the evening. Considering he hadn't had an erection since before the accident, he could hardly believe his body's responsiveness. He prayed like hell she didn't look down.

And then she did.

Christ!

A wicked gleam entered her cornflower-colored eyes, and her sweet smile transformed into a wicked grin. He remembered her mischievous expressions well. The look promised him that before the night's end, he'd be begging for mercy.

The tent in his pants expanded another inch when she licked her lips. He longed for the days of old when he could scoop her over his shoulder, smack her ass, and take her to bed. That frisky activity would likely never happen between them again, and the knowledge made him moody as hell.

"I'm not into pity fucks, Claire," he snapped.

A wary mask settled on her features, and he cursed his wayward tongue.

Where the hell had that come from? And what the hell was wrong with him? She'd been ready to polish his knob, and he had to go and spoil it. Why was it every time they were within two feet of each other, he had to ruin the mood? To kill her glimmering spark?

"I should go," she whispered tearfully.

As she moved to pass him, he captured her hand and drew her onto his lap. The pain of her hipbone connecting with his dick was penance, or so he told himself. When he could speak again, after his discomfort eased, he begged her forgiveness.

"I'm an ass. I...I hate everything about this chair and what it represents. When you look at me with desire in your eyes, I have a hard time believing it's real." He swallowed and stroked her petal-soft cheek. "I can't believe you could ever want me like this—broken. Half the man I used to be."

She remained silent. Watchful. And he swallowed his rising anguish.

"I'm sorry, Claire. The twisted part of my mind believes your enthusiasm is an act. That you want so badly for things to return to normal, maybe you're just going through the motions of wanting me because you believe it's what I want, too. Because you feel sorry for me or guilty," he confessed hoarsely.

For the longest time, he focused on the wedding ring he couldn't bring himself to remove. He snorted in self-disgust. If he were being honest with himself, his grip on her hip was a lifeline. She needed freedom from his tow line, or she'd be dragged down by him yet again.

Finger by finger, he eased his hold. When she didn't bolt

away, he raised his head to meet her gaze. He gulped at the fire in her eyes. It had nothing to do with ardor and everything to do with rage.

Claire was beautiful on any given day, with or without makeup, dressed in designer clothes or sweats. But this furious version was a sight to behold. Blazing eyes, heightened color, and the fierce passion all equaled perfection. A vengeful angel in the flesh.

His dick stood at its full height, waving like a pageant queen on parade. No doubt she felt it, knocking against her hip, begging for her attention.

"When have you ever known me to lie, Declan?"

Her tone was cold and clipped. Should he take it as encouragement that she didn't slap his face or sail out the door?

"Do you honestly think I would pity fuck you? *Really?* Because if you honestly believe it, then it isn't just your back that's broken. It's your dumbass brain."

With those words, the cracks in his heart fused together, and he grinned in relief.

Her eyes grew stormier, and her brows dipped lower. His stupid-ass smile inched wider. Reaching up, he cupped a breast through her thin shirt, brushing a thumb over the hardened nipple her demi bra did nothing to hide.

She knocked his hand away, rose, and stalked into the bedroom. As if leashed with no will of his own, he rolled after her. He paused in the entry, watching with held breath as she whipped off her shirt and shimmied out of her shorts.

Dear God, she was gorgeous!

Lose the bra, lose the bra, he silently chanted, sighing his relief as she reached for the fastening.

"So we're having angry sex?" he asked hopefully.

Her arms dropped to her sides, and she curled her fists in frustration. "We aren't having any sex, you blockhead."

Leaving her underwear on—and wasn't it a damned shame?—she climbed into bed and jerked the covers up to her neck. He nearly chortled with glee when she forgot to put the friendship pillow in place.

The idea of toying with her, of playing the helpless male needing her to assist him into bed, teased his brain. It would allow him to cop another feel, maybe get a face full of luscious tatas when she leaned over him. The only thing keeping him from going there was his pride. Appearing pathetic, fake or otherwise, didn't sit well with him.

Stripping down, he hauled himself onto the mattress. A glance down showed his dick had no intention of relaxing to its normal state—not without help. If he didn't know better, he'd suspect someone had slipped a little blue pill into his drink.

"Sweetheart?"

"What?"

"I have a bit of a problem."

She half sat and cast him a concerned look. It only took her a second to register his nude form on top of the comforter. Her eyes narrowed on his hard shaft. Lips compressed, she continued to stare. Declan waited with bated breath.

When she bit her lower lip, he knew he had her. Twinkling blue eyes lifted to meet his gaze. "It's not a 'bit of a problem.' It's a pretty *big* problem."

"Only if we don't take care of it right away," he quipped. Though in reality, he was more than a little serious. Blue balls *could* be an issue.

"Never let it be said I didn't do my part to help."

Her head dipped, and his eyes rolled back in his head. The feel of her warm mouth convinced him he'd died and gone to heaven. When her hand cupped his balls, he was sure of it. With one hand fisted in her hair and the other tucked behind his head, he watched her pleasure him. And as the pressure built, before he could shoot off, she paused to smirk up at him.

Declan knew that look! Claire was about to negotiate. And she'd get her way. She always did.

"Whatever you are about to demand, consider it a yes," he growled, tightening the fingers in her hair.

She giggled, and his dick jumped in time to the musical cadence of her laughter.

Pounding on the front door interrupted whatever she'd intended to say.

"Who the hell is banging on the door at midnight?" he asked.

Claire sat up, worry apparent.

"I suppose we have to see who it is?" he asked, half ready to weep in frustration.

She drew on her discarded shirt as he dragged on his trousers.

He'd transferred into his chair and wheeled halfway into the living room as she opened the door. Looming there, six feet plus of pissed-off male, was the red-faced Thomas.

CHAPTER 6

Claire cringed when Thomas's eyes swept over them. With the hem of her top barely reaching the top of her thighs and Declan sans his shirt with his pants unbuttoned, the picture was clear. She experienced a pang of regret for hurting Thomas this way, but Declan was her all. Or he had been. And his transition to his old self was irresistible.

Thomas lifted his fist, and the crinkle of paper was overly loud in the silence. He crumpled it into a tight ball and flung it on the ground. "This is all I get? No in-person explanation?"

"Let me guess," said Declan in a sardonic voice. "You were showering, and when you finished, there was no Claire. In place of her suitcase was a goodbye note. How'd I do?"

Blood rushed to her cheeks, and she shot him an accusing glare. His carefully blank expression was worrisome.

"Is this some kind of sick game the two of you concocted?" Thomas asked with barely contained rage. "You find a poor unsuspecting idiot and get them to pay for your vacation, then stick it to them?"

All friendly camaraderie left Declan.

"Watch it, friend. You're treading on thin ice," he warned. The steely quality in his words sent a shiver down Claire's spine. Even in a wheelchair, he was an imposing figure, wielding power with only his voice and a look. "There's no endgame here. Claire never expected me to be on the island, nor did I expect to run into her. The note? Yeah, I got the same the day she left me."

"I didn't ask you to pay for everything, Thomas. You—"

Declan cut her off. Pinning her with his intense, dark gaze, he said, "Choose. Here and now."

Panic welled within her, making it difficult to breathe. Frozen in place, she was unable to utter a single sound. If she picked Declan, she risked him regressing to the surly bastard he'd been since that fateful January. Her heart wanted to take a chance on him, yet her head told her Thomas was the safer bet.

But she didn't love him.

And a second rejection from Declan would kill her ability to fall in love again. Was it too much to ask for a crystal ball?

"As if I'd take her back now," Thomas snarled. "She's no better than a—"

Seeing Declan's instantaneous fury halted the insult. Or perhaps it was when he surged up from the chair and took four steps that shocked them into immobility. Their surprised expressions finally registered with him, and he checked his forward motion.

"What the fuck are you staring at?" he snapped.

"You're standing," Claire croaked.

He frowned and glanced down. Stunned disbelief transformed his face, and he seemed suddenly fearful of moving.

Unexpected tears and incredulous laughter poured out of her. She wanted so badly to bask in the joy associated with his walking, but also sob because it had taken him becoming enraged over her lousy life choices to do it.

"Oh, Declan!" She flung her arms around him, rejoicing as he clasped her tightly in return.

"Claire, I walked," he said hoarsely.

"Yes," she sobbed. "Oh, Declan," she said again, too overcome to articulate her relief at seeing him walk.

Thomas put aside his anger at the miracle of the moment. Or maybe he finally understood she would never love anyone as completely as she did her husband. Regardless, he exited the cabana.

She didn't know how long they stood embracing, but without warning, Declan's legs began trembling—a slight muscle twitch at first, progressing into shaking. Claire rushed to grab his chair.

"No," he said, and then staggered his way to the sofa. He collapsed onto the cushion with a heavy sigh.

"How will you get to bed if you don't use the chair, Declan? I can't support your body weight."

"I'll sleep here tonight. You take the bed."

His voice possessed an odd quality, and she hated how triggered she felt.

"What did I do wrong this time?"

"Nothing. You did nothing wrong, but I won't be anyone's consolation prize, Claire. If you want to be with your boyfriend, go to him."

"What are you talking about?" she asked, bewildered.

She tried to touch his arm, but he jerked as if burned. "Do you have a screw loose?"

"I asked you to choose," he explained in an aching voice, and it didn't take a genius to understand her hesitation had hurt him. He confirmed it. "I asked you to choose, and when you looked at me, I could see the doubt. The panic. Yes, he's the safer bet. I get it. Although I don't particularly like the way he spoke to you. But if you truly care for him, I won't stand in your way."

"Stand in my way?" she asked woodenly.

"The divorce, Claire. I'll sign whatever you want. I won't contest it."

She fought to contain her frustration. Not ten minutes ago, they were in bed, her mouth on him, ready to reaffirm their love—or so she thought—and now he was ready to cast her aside? All because she'd been momentarily crippled by insecurity?

Cold invaded her body, and she welcomed the numbing sensation it brought. She wasn't sure what she'd been thinking by coming here. But she could finally acknowledge it had been a mistake of epic proportions.

Wordlessly, she left him to seek her solace. Once in the bedroom, she stared at the rumpled bed and wondered how she'd ever sleep. Peeling off the sheet and grabbing a pillow, she offered them up to Declan.

As she spun on her heel to leave, he called out.

"Claire."

Although it paused her retreat, she couldn't—wouldn't—look at him.

"What?"

"I'm sorry if my coming to the island disrupted your plans."

It was on the tip of her tongue to say, "Me too." But she wasn't sorry. Inasmuch as this moment was shredding her soul, seeing the ghost of the man she'd once loved walk those few short steps wasn't something she'd trade for keeping her soul intact. Her heart had been broken many, many times over, and she could patch it together again, just like before. And if that pesky organ wasn't quite as shiny and new as it had once been, no one was the wiser but herself.

Sleep was an elusive bitch. A kaleidoscope of images played over and over through her mind. She glanced at the bedside clock.

Three a.m.

Was it possible to add up all the sleepless nights she'd had since her perfect world had shattered? Probably not, although they most likely outnumbered the ones with fitful rest.

The sliding glass doors off the bedroom beckoned. A walk along the beach was exactly what she needed to clear her head and relax. Claire rose, drew on her shorts, and slipped on a pair of flip-flops.

She considered telling Declan, but if he was sleeping, she didn't want to disturb him. Soundlessly, she opened the door and breathed in the fresh sea breeze. As she strolled the empty shoreline, shoes in hand, she could feel each of the day's little horrors fall into place like a puzzle piece, giving her perspective.

Her toes curled in the warm sand, and she was surprised it retained the heat from the day. Maybe she should relocate to Florida or California, buy a condo, and spend her evenings haunting the beach, detoxing from each day's events.

The hairs on the back of her neck prickled, standing on end—her early warning system. Not early enough. As she whirled around to see what had inspired her danger radar, rough hands grabbed her and shoved a gag in her mouth. Next came a hood over her head, then all went black.

As the night wore on, Declan called himself a hundred kinds of fool for pissing her off. As he replayed the evening over, recalling her deer-in-the-headlights expression, he understood her actions for what they were.

Fear.

Of him.

Of his unpredictable and potentially explosive responses.

It pained him.

In the morning, he'd see if Claire would have breakfast with him and discuss what a future together might look like. Sure, she might tell him to go to hell, but he had to apologize and make one last attempt to win her back. She'd loved him once. A deep connection like theirs didn't simply disappear, right? If they could clear the air once and for all, they might power through the hurt and find a way forward.

For the third time that night, a banging sounded on his door. A glance at his watch showed it to be just after three a.m.

What the hell?

"It's like fucking Grand Central Station," he growled.

If Thomas had returned, Declan held a throat punch with the guy's name on it. Or maybe a ball punch, since the confines of his wheelchair didn't allow him to reach the cover-model wannabe's neck.

On colt-like legs, he staggered to his chair and sat down heavily. He cast a speculative look at the closed bedroom door. Why hadn't Claire charged out with all the noise? Odd.

A haggard-looking Gavin with Alejandro Reyes wasn't what he'd expected.

"What's going on? Is everything okay?"

"Bonnie's missing," Gavin said, a tremble in his voice, his hands shaking like a recovering alcoholic on his first day of rehab. Declan could relate to the mental analogy. "Have you heard from her, D.?"

"No. Missing? What the fuck? What do you mean by missing?" Declan couldn't wrap his sleep-deprived mind around it.

"When I returned to our cabana, we argued some more, and she stormed out. I figured she needed to cool off, but she didn't return." Gavin scrubbed his scalp, frustration pouring off him in waves. "After a little time had passed, I started to get worried. You know Bonnie, she can stay mad for all of an hour, if that."

"How long has she been gone?"

"Since around midnight, as best we can tell," Alejandro cut in. "We thought we'd check with Mrs. Braddock to see if she might know where her friend would go."

Declan once again frowned toward the closed bedroom door. There was no possible way Claire would have slept through this commotion. Of the two of them, she was the lighter sleeper. It couldn't have changed much in their five-month separation.

"Claire!" he yelled, wheeling as fast as he could toward the bedroom. "Claire!"

He flung open the door to find the room abandoned. He checked the adjoining bathroom. Empty. The unlocked glass doors told the tale.

"She's gone," he said to no one. The words were spoken softly on an expelled breath. She'd snuck out without a word to him. He hung his head as the pain struck. The fact that she'd prefer to slink out the back door rather than speak to him weighed heavily on his soul. As he spun toward Gavin and Alejandro, standing in the doorway, he noticed Claire's suitcase in the corner.

The truth clicked in.

She wouldn't have left for good without her clothing.

Relief surged through him. Perhaps she'd gone for a walk on the beach? If so, when had she left?

Alejandro's gaze touched on the case. "Not permanently. My staff and I will search the beach. Stay here in case she returns. Keep this radio with you, and I'll check in soon."

"Do you think they're together?" Gavin asked after Alejandro left.

"I don't see how. I wasn't sleeping and would've heard Bonnie knock on the slider. For that matter, why wouldn't she have used the front door?"

Stealing away Gavin's hope the two women were safely holed up, having a drink or bitching about their men, didn't feel all that great. But the reality was that both women were not where they should be, and it was cause for concern.

Declan and Gavin's wait was interminable. Neither spoke as they listened to the voices on the radio break the intolerable silence now and again.

"Boss, looks like signs of a struggle, not far from the Gardner cabana."

"Yes, I found the same in this location," Alejandro's accented voice replied grimly, before switching to rapid Spanish.

Gavin and Declan shared a horrified look when they heard the one word they understood.

Pirates!

CHAPTER 7

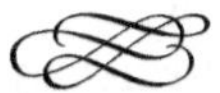

$\mathcal{U}$nder her thick, black hood, Claire's ability to hear or see was severely diminished. Terror clawed her stomach, making her want to vomit or pass out. Or both. Who would kidnap her from an exclusive island resort beach in the wee hours of the morning?

Someone looking to ransom her? Perhaps, if they mistakenly believed she had money.

Sex traffickers? Didn't they tend to target younger, more attractive women?

Regret hit her hard.

Declan.

He'd never know what had happened to her. He'd lose someone else and blame himself as he had with their son. She prayed he wouldn't spiral down as he had before. God, why hadn't she told him she loved him still, with every cell of her body, every fiber of her being? If she lived a thousand years, her feelings would never change.

Her abductors seemed to have reached their destination, shuffling her through a door and tossing her none too gently onto a plush mattress. The sack was torn off her head, snagging a few stray strands of hair in the process.

Her muffled "Oww!" didn't affect the man standing before her.

And holy shit, what a man!

A perfect specimen who clearly worked out regularly, or maybe it was the physical act of hauling captive women that had his legs the size of tree trunks and his arms… whoa, those arms!

Her mouth watered as she looked her fill.

A mermaid tattoo snaked up his forearm and curled around his bicep. The color was brilliant in the design, and the aquamarine eyes of the siren were mesmerizing. The fact that he was flexing those muscles could also be why she was transfixed.

"You like?" His deep, amused voice wrapped around her and warmed the parts of her body that in no way should be so turned on. Perhaps the desire was left over from her earlier sexual frustration with Declan.

She looked up into eyes as bright as those in the tattoo.

Holy fuck!

Well, if she had to be abducted, being snatched by someone resembling the superhero Thor was the way to go. Could she help it if her sex-starved self prompted her to reach out and caress his massive chest? Her tied hands only made the contrast of her thin wrists and his sizable muscles hotter.

Yeah, she liked, but she'd cut out her tongue before admitting it.

The door swung open, and Bonnie sailed into the room, a huge, shit-eating grin on her face. "Welcome aboard, matey!" Her piss-poor imitation of the pirate lingo left a lot to be desired.

"Bonnie? What the hell is going on?"

"It's our fantasy to be captured by hot pirates," Bonnie replied. Excitement bubbled off her.

"Do Declan and Gavin know about this? And when did I sign up for the "pirate" fantasy?" Bewildered didn't begin to describe Claire's state of mind.

"It's what these Elysian Island vacations are based on—fantasies. Whatever you can imagine, they have. Don't you remember me asking, 'If you could create the perfect dreamworld, what might it be?'"

"Well, yeah, but I thought it was girl talk. Like, if you were hiring a male strip-o-gram for my birthday, how would I want him to dress, kind of thing. I didn't think you would have me abducted and scared witless," Claire groused.

Bonnie continued to smile in the face of her ire.

"You do realize I have a boyfriend, *and* a husband, right?" When the pirate snorted and Bonnie laughed, Claire realized how it sounded. She glanced up into the pirate's twinkling eyes. "I didn't mean it like that."

"We don't judge, *mi tesoro,*" he murmured, shifting closer.

"Yeah, you probably shouldn't be assigning me pet names."

"Isn't he perfect?" Bonnie sighed.

Claire had to admit he was—all six-foot-six of him. She held up her bound wrists. "Do you mind?"

"Actually, I do. You will stay tied, *mi tesoro.*" Mr. Tall, Tanned, and Dangerous pushed her back on the bed and knotted the excess rope through an iron ring attached to the wall.

"*What?* No! Bonnie, do something!"

Horror filled her when her friend's eyes widened, as if shocked by his actions. Perhaps she saw this kinky fantasy abduction going differently. How far was the staff allowed to push things here on the island?

Once he'd secured her to the wall, he bent to scoop Bonnie over his shoulder. No amount of struggling or pounding on his back slowed him down as he hauled her out the door. If they got out of this unharmed, a strongly worded letter to management was in order.

"What the hell do you mean *pirates?*" Declan raged. "Have you called the authorities? What are you doing to find my wife?"

Alejandro didn't appear threatened by Declan's anger. The fact made him all the more livid. He cast a look at Gavin who sat on the sofa, shell-shocked. His friend hadn't said a word since they'd heard the resort owner address the staff over the radio. What the hell was going on here?

"It appears your wives listed being abducted by 'hot pirates' as their greatest wish," Alejandro explained, looking at a printout before him. "Your agenda, along with Mr. Gardner's, is to rescue them from where they are being held captive."

"What the fuck are you talking about?" Declan yelled. He gestured to his chair. "Does it look like I planned to be running about the island looking for clues on how to save a woman I didn't even know would be here? What type of twisted con game are you running here?"

Gavin's head whipped up, and he fixed Declan with his stare. "Bonnie."

"Bonnie what?"

"She asked yesterday if we'd read the brochures. We admitted we didn't. Remember? She had to have signed us up for this."

"What in God's name was she thinking?"

Gavin shook his head, seemingly bewildered.

"Tell me they're at least safe," Declan demanded.

Alejandro held out a paper with a map of what appeared to be a compound and pointed to a large X. "The women are being held here. I'm sorry to report, it's a lawless island off Elysian Island's southwesternmost point. I have an elite team of ex-SEALs who specialize in extracting guests captured by that particular band of pirates. I *will* say Captain Rodrigo is a wildcard."

"This keeps getting better." Declan shook his head. "Why is he a wildcard?"

"If he likes your woman, he'll keep her."

"You've got to be shitting me?"

"No, I promise, I am not 'shitting' you. It is why we employ the retired SEAL team to rescue the women foolish enough to sign up for my associate Mario's program. They are usually able to get them back safely with little bloodshed."

Declan scrubbed his hands up and down his face.

This was a living nightmare. He must've fallen into a dream he'd yet to wake from, because in real life, these things didn't happen. A man's wife didn't get abducted by a pirate captain named Rodrigo, who may or may not decide he wants to keep her. No one signed up to go to an island where they longed for this kind of warped excitement. And more importantly, a best friend's wife didn't sign up a wheelchair-bound man to go on a physical rescue mission to retrieve his soon-to-be ex-wife.

Laughter, inappropriate and hysterical in nature, exploded from him. Unable to stop the chortling and tears of mirth, Declan bent double and wiped his eyes. Oh, the gang at his weekly AA meeting would love the hell out of this story.

"I suggest you both try to get some sleep. I'll assemble the team in the morning," their host informed them.

The idea that either of them could sleep had Declan laughing longer and harder.

Without warning, he sobered and glared at Gavin. "When we get them back safely, I'm going to murder your wife."

"Get in line," Gavin muttered.

CHAPTER 8

Claire imagined most women would undoubtedly adore a shredded beast of a man attempting to feed them. However, she wasn't one of them. Or at least she didn't appreciate it when she was being held captive against her will.

Rodrigo, as he'd informed her his name was, traced the outline of her compressed lips with a chocolate-covered strawberry. "Come, *mi tesoro*, you must eat."

She snapped her teeth at his finger, missing by mere centimeters.

"Go to the devil," she spat, with a kick in his direction for good measure.

He ignored her outburst and clapped his hands.

If she didn't know any better, Claire would've thought she'd stepped back in time. In came servants dressed in similar period garb to the ship's captain. The serving maids never looked up from dumping water into the hip bath. How did they bend and still breathe in those blasted corsets?

"You shall have a bath. Keira has found you a dress and clean undergarments," he informed her.

Suddenly, it became apparent to her—the man was Crazy with a capital C. "You're cracked in the head."

Pique lit those unsettling aquamarine eyes. "You will do as you're told, wench."

"Nice to see I've been downgraded from your treasure to wench. Maybe soon you'll let me go."

"No. You are my woman now."

A snort of incredulous laughter escaped her. "Never going to happen, Captain Oblivious. I'm married."

"Yes, with a boyfriend. I know. What you fail to realize is this is *my* island. Here I am in charge. You will come to accept your fate soon enough."

"Look, I'm sure you and your island of misfit toys would appeal to some, but not me. I can promise you, first chance I get, I'll stab you in the heart. Save yourself some grief. Let me and my friend go."

He crowded her against the wall, running his large, rough hand down to the base of her throat. "No, *mi tesoro*. You will be mine."

Had he not been so impassioned, so imposing, she would have rolled her eyes. As it was, she found it difficult to look away from the mesmerizing light glowing so brightly in his gaze. If there was no Declan, she would have promptly forgotten Thomas and lived with this crackpot in paradise. He was compelling, no doubt. But she loved her husband. The long hours during the night spent listening to this beefy Latino snore while in his drunken state had made clear exactly what she wanted.

"Come, you will bathe," Rodrigo declared.

"Not with you in the room, I won't," she retorted.

His wicked grin caused her insides to churn. She wondered for the thousandth time why Bonnie had thought being held prisoner by a lunatic who dressed like he was from the eighteenth century had possibly been a good idea.

"Such passion! Ah, you will surely warm my bed tonight."

"I think you can warm you own damned bed just fine without me. Build a fire if you're cold."

The idea of a fire on board the ship appalled him, and his expression was one of horror. "Look around you, my love. This wood is flammable. The ship would go up in flames within minutes."

Claire frowned.

"What? Do you not believe me?"

"Why did your accent disappear?"

His grin bloomed ear to ear. "Ah, busted. It's hard to stay in character at the idea of all this going up in a puff of smoke."

"Character? So this *is* all an act? You aren't a real pirate?"

"Yes and no." He waved away the serving maids and draped himself across the bunk as much as his large frame would allow, propping his head in his hand. "It's a partial act. The sloop is real. I had it restored about two years ago when I found it off the coast of my island."

"Your island? We aren't on Elysian Island anymore?"

"No."

"What gives you the right to kidnap unsuspecting women from the beach? What if I had medication I needed back in my room?" Her rage boiled beneath the surface.

"The right is a contract from Alejandro Reyes. There were two of you who had filled out paperwork stating you wished this to be your fantasy. As for the other inconsequential issue… again, Alejandro or Thalia provided the background information on you. I know you don't need any medication."

"Really, smartass? What about my birth control pills?"

She could see that her question surprised him.

"Do you ever think of those things when you're out snatching and seducing women? How many little Rodrigo clones do you think are running around right now?"

He paled, and his complexion took on a green hue.

"I can see you never gave it a second thought. Now cut me loose. I'm losing feeling in my damned arms."

Suddenly, he was all charm again. "You've made it obvious you've been thinking about sex with me. I have condoms."

Claire kicked him square in the stomach. The pain radiated up her leg, and she shook her head. Damn the man and his abs of steel!

"What was that for?" he demanded, sitting up and shifting out of reach.

"I am not now—*nor ever*—having sex with you."

"Can't blame a guy for trying."

"Yes. I. Can," she said through gritted teeth.

"I'll be back when you're in a better frame of mind."

Standing, he pulled his shirt over his head and strode to a built-in closet on the other side of the cabin. He opened the wardrobe door to reveal a half dozen more billowing white shirts, all identical to the one he'd discarded.

Curiosity got the better of her. "How long have you been doing this? Is it a popular fantasy?"

His booming laugh left her in little doubt. "Since the resort opened. And you tell me." With that, he spread his arms wide and showcased his mouthwatering torso with a slow spin worthy of a catwalk model.

Yes, it was definitely popular.

"How does this all end? How do I get back?"

"When I decide you no longer amuse me. *Or* you're rescued by the man of your choosing."

He whipped on a clean shirt, winked, and exited, leaving her alone with her disturbing thoughts. The man of her choosing would be Declan, but it would be a cold day in hell if he ever came after her. Thomas either. Maybe she should make nice with Captain Oblivious. She might be in for a very long stay.

She swore savagely when she realized he'd distracted her with his chest and never untied her.

Ten hours had passed since the women had disappeared, and Declan was about to blow a gasket. While Gavin and the rescue team prepared for their stealth attack, he'd gone in search of Thomas. Alejandro made it clear Captain Rodrigo might release Claire if he believed there was true love involved. Personally, Declan thought it was a crock of shit, but he was willing to set aside his animosity for Thomas if the other man did his best to rescue Claire.

Declan found him coming down the path leading to his personal cabana. As Thomas moved to go around him, he used his wheelchair to cut him off and stopped the guy's forward progress. For a moment they stared at one another, each unsure what to say to the other.

"Claire's been taken," Declan finally blurted.

"Taken? By who?" Thomas instantly became concerned.

His worry spoke well of him, and Declan decided Claire could do worse than a guy who genuinely seemed to care.

"They believe it was by a pirate who calls himself Captain Rodrigo."

A frown drew Thomas's brows together. "Hey man, are you all right? I mean, did you mix up your meds or something?"

Rolling his eyes, Declan huffed out a breath. "Oh for fuc—yes, I'm fine," he ground out. "I need you to follow me to Alejandro's office. We've got a plan to get Claire and Bonnie back, but we may require your help."

"Wait! Bonnie, too? Where is Gavin?"

"In Alejandro's office," Declan said slowly, as if he were speaking to the slowest patient in the psych ward.

"You don't have to be a dick about it. But please *do* explain to me why I should go out of my way to help a woman who ran away in the middle of the night," Thomas challenged, arms crossed against his burly chest.

"Because it's the decent thing to do," Declan growled, slamming his hands down on the armrests. Reining in his building frustration and simmering rage, he said, "Please, Thomas. Help me get her back. I realize you don't owe either of us a damned thing, but I will owe *you* if you do this for me now."

The silence stretched out, and Declan imagined Thomas was weighing the consequences and whether he cared enough to put his neck on the line. Just when Declan thought he'd go mad, Thomas agreed, all animosity gone.

"Okay. I'll do whatever I can. Lead the way."

"Thank you."

"I'm not doing it for you. I'm doing it for *her.* You've put her through a lot, Braddock. When you should've been comforting her on the loss of her child, you wallowed in your own self-pity. She deserves better than you."

Although Declan wanted to bite Thomas's head off, the guy was correct. She did deserve better. With a nod, Declan wheeled around and rolled toward the direction of the main building.

CHAPTER 9

"According to our intel, Rodrigo has the women on his ship just off the coast of Ram Rod Island. They're in separate cabins, and there's no way to approach without being spotted."

The head of Alpha Team was far too calm for Declan's tastes. The entire outfit was pretty laid back except for the mild undercurrent of excitement, most likely from the impending mission. He'd met two Navy SEALS in his life, and even after retirement, they craved excitement. Adrenaline junkies, the lot of them.

"Ram Rod Island?" Declan scoffed in disbelief before holding up a hand and shaking his head. "Never mind, I'm sure I don't want to know."

"Sounds like the guy is overcompensating if you ask me," Thomas inserted. "Is this Captain Rodrigo looking for a ransom? Is this a shakedown?"

The questions were valid, and as one, they all looked to Alejandro.

"I promise you, it is not," their host said. "As I stated earlier, this is what your women signed your group up for. We allow it to play out as long as the women aren't in serious danger."

Clearly Thomas had never read the brochure either, and it made Declan happy to know the guy wasn't so perfect.

"So what happens if the team can't get to the boat? How do we retrieve Bonnie and Claire?" Gavin voiced the worry that was utmost on Declan's mind.

"We'll still approach in a Zodiac, but we'll come up behind the ship, staying out of cannon range," Mac Becker, A-Team leader extraordinaire, explained. As the person overseeing this rescue, his matter-of-fact explanations gave Declan a semblance of comfort, making him feel marginally better about what would happen.

"You've all done this before with this Rodrigo character, I'm assuming. None of you appears to be concerned. Why is that?" Declan asked. "Is it because this is part of the fantasy game? Or is this pirate not a real threat?"

"Oh, he's a real threat," Thalia said, seemingly materializing from thin air.

Declan, Gavin, and Thomas jumped in surprise, but her sudden appearance didn't seem to startle anyone else. She must've been expected.

"But the people signing up for this type of adventure aren't technically being taken against their will. Because he's not stealing anything of value, law enforcement turns a blind eye," she said with a casual shrug.

Thalia laid a comforting hand on Declan's shoulder, and he would swear he felt a calming energy run through his body. It made him uncomfortable, yet at the same time, energized and ready to conquer the world. Certainly, it was all his imagination. No one could possess the ability to alter another's mind. Still, he found it hard to deny what he was experiencing.

"So why the general lack of concern?" Gavin reiterated the question.

"He can be reasoned with ninety-nine percent of the time," Alejandro said with a careless shrug.

"And the other one percent?" Declan didn't like that they weren't giving the situation the seriousness he felt it deserved. He was two seconds away from savagely tearing someone's head off their shoulders—with his teeth.

"Mr. Braddock, we need you to trust that we'll get the women back safely. Can you do that?" Thalia asked, portraying a tranquility Declan was far from feeling. Gavin, too, if the frustrated look on his face was any sign of his inner turmoil.

Declan slowly shook his head. This situation was utterly unbelievable. Had anyone told him this had happened to *their* wife, he'd have asked what drug cocktail they'd consumed. Yet here he sat, frustrated beyond measure, with Claire's current boyfriend across from him, making him uncomfortable with a probing stare.

Why the hell wasn't Thomas losing his shit?

Unable to tolerate the confines of his chair another moment, when he was ready to come out of his skin, he locked his wheels and stood. The surprised looks he received didn't faze him. Minus Thomas, they'd all believed he was paralyzed. On shaky legs, he wobbled to stand next to Gavin and rested his hands on the table. "Let's go over the plan again," he said gruffly.

"Yo! Captain Oblivious!" Claire shouted, squirming to ease the discomfort of her bladder. "Hey! Anybody out there? When I get free, I'm going to sink this piece of sh—."

The door slammed open, cutting through her threat. "What is it, wench?"

Claire gaped at the man standing in the entry. Holy hell! Each pirate was hotter than the last on this ship. "Who are y-you?"

"Bram. First mate to Captain Rodrigo. What do you want? What's with all the caterwauling?"

Heat flooded her face at being forced to discuss her body functions with a stranger. "I have to go to the bathroom."

His cold eyes raked her from head to toe before settling back on her face. "Why haven't you made use of the chamber pot?"

Claire's brows drew together in confusion. Did he not see she was still tied? She held up her bound wrists with a challenging brow. "Duh."

He squinted his ire at her and spun to leave.

"Hey! Matey! What part of 'I have to go to the bathroom' didn't you get?"

"I intended to find another female to assist you. But talk to me in that manner again, and I'll gag you, letting you wallow in your own filth. Got it?" His tone almost gave her frostbite.

Mutely, she nodded, even though his back was to her. As audible as her gulp was, he'd certainly heard her fear. Apparently, First Mate Bram woke up on the wrong side of the bed today.

"I can't hear you."

She shivered and snapped a resentful, "Yes."

After a sharp inclination of his head, he was off, leaving her to fight back tears. This was not the vacation she'd envisioned by any stretch of the imagination.

A young woman with silver-blonde hair, bearing a striking resemblance to Thalia, walked in. Were they related? If so, could she be persuaded to send a message to the resort owners? Or more importantly, what constituted authorities in this area of the world?

Claire's hope built. She looked beyond the woman's shoulder to ascertain if they were alone.

Lowering her voice, she asked, "Do you know Thalia from Elysian Island?"

When the stranger glanced behind her, she exposed the ruined side of her face, which, until that moment, had been hidden by her hair.

Claire gasped at the jagged scar running from temple to jaw, and the other woman refused to meet her gaze, hanging her head lower. Immediately, Claire regretted her unforgivable reaction to something so superficial as a scar, but she'd been surprised the puckered mark appeared recent and angry.

"Please," Claire whispered urgently. "You must get her a message for me if you know her. Will you help me?"

Again, the woman ignored her, refusing to speak.

Gripping the work-worn hands untying her, Claire said, "I know you can understand me. Please. This isn't a game."

"She won't help you," Bram's frosty voice cut in. "She's my wife and does what she's told."

Her heart sank. If she'd been married to that devil, she probably wouldn't disobey him either. Raising her chin, she cut him an evil look. "Listen, McSwagger. If you're abusing her in any way, I'll castrate you."

His mouth twitched, and a glimmer of respect shone brightly from his ice-blue eyes. She received the feeling that her threat amused him greatly. Yet she meant it. She wouldn't abide abuse.

"Duly noted." His tone softened when he addressed his wife, "Keira, bring her up on deck to stretch her legs when she's finished."

After he departed, Claire met Keira's sparkling eyes.

"He adores you, doesn't he?"

With a wink, Keira left her free to do her business.

Claire was an idiot. This entire "abduction" was an act, and she needed to remember it. It wasn't easy when it felt so real. Although, when she tried the knob to leave, she found it locked, leaving her with no idea what to believe at that point.

She paced around the cabin, happy for the freedom of movement, but impatient to get fresh air. Rodrigo's cologne wasn't offensive, but it tended to overwhelm the space.

When the door opened for the third time in fifteen minutes, she whirled toward the sound, expecting to see Keira.

"Hello, *mi tesoro*. Have you missed me today?" Captain Rodrigo purred.

Would it be wrong to confess to missing his chest?

"No," she snapped. "Where's Bonnie? I'm done with this stupid game. I want to go back to my husband. *Right now!*"

"The gimp?" Rodrigo immediately dropped his accent along with the act, all pretense of manners gone.

Her rage was immediate and all-consuming. She flew at

him, claws bared, ready to draw blood. "Don't you *dare* call him that! He's ten times the man you'll *ever* be!"

He caught her wrists in one hand as if she were no more than a bothersome child.

"Hmm. We'll see." And with those words, he ground his mouth against hers, seeking entrance with his tongue.

She promptly bit him.

"Sonofabitch!" He drew back and touched a thumb to his bleeding lip. "What is *wrong* with you?"

"I don't like being manhandled."

"Ah, are you moody because the gimp can't get it up?"

She slapped him so hard that *her* ears rang. Narrow-eyed, his cold expression chilled her to the bone. Perhaps she'd gone too far. The red, angry imprint of her hand on his cheek almost made her feel bad.

Time stood still as they sized each other up.

A frantic shout from above deck broke their staring contest, and he swung around, rushing to discover the cause. Claire, of course, was hot on his heels.

The crew was crowded together, surrounded by what looked to be a military team. Or it could be the militia. She only hoped they were here to rescue her and not serve her another crap topping on top of her shit sandwich.

"Claire!"

Declan's voice floated up from far below the railing.

"Declan!" she shouted.

When she rushed toward the side, Rodrigo grabbed her around the waist and placed a large Bowie knife against the column of her throat.

"I don't think so, *mi tesoro*. I told you, you're mine." His low voice next to her ear sent a shiver down her spine.

"Let her go, Rodrigo."

The command came from the head of the rescue team, yet Claire focused solely on the man stepping onto the deck. His jerky movements spoke of his screaming muscles, and the urge to assist him, to help ease his discomfort, was overpowering.

She cried out when he stumbled.

"Seems the gimp is determined to get you back," Rodrigo commented casually as if he didn't hold a sharp instrument against her carotid artery.

"When I'm free, I'm going to stab you with your fucking knife," she returned coldly.

"Yes, yes," he said dismissively. "So you've threatened before. Such a bloodthirsty woman. You'll make the perfect pirate's wench," he told her warmly.

"You're cracked in the melon," she retorted.

He palmed her head in his oversized hand and ran his tongue up the side of her face. "Deny it all you will, *mi tesoro*, but we both know you want me."

Declan had paused to rest against the rail, but upon seeing Rodrigo touch her, whispering intimately, he surged forward, indignation vibrating from every pore. A secret part of her was thrilled that he'd taken umbrage at another man's hands on her.

"Let her go, you sonofabitch," Declan snarled.

"Hello, gimp. Come to retrieve your wayward wife?"

She'd had enough. "I told you not to call him that!"

Slamming her elbow into his ribcage, Claire simultaneously stomped on his instep.

Though he grunted, he held on tight.

"Nice try, *mi tesoro*. But I'm not Captain for nothing," he said with a roguish chuckle.

"Jesus Christ, it's like I'm stuck in a badly written play," she complained.

Somewhere, someone laughed, and she searched for the culprit. Thomas stood just beyond Declan, struggling to contain his hilarity. What he found funny about this situation was far beyond her comprehension, but he wasn't gaining any brownie points.

Gavin was the last to board the ship. His eyes sought and found Bonnie, held on the far side of the mast, in the clutches of a very unamused Bram. Indecision flashed across Gavin's features as if he were uncertain if his wife wanted to see him. His relief was humbling as her captor released her, and she ran straight into Gavin's arms.

Claire moved her head marginally, very much aware Rodrigo still held the blade to her throat. Declan never removed his fierce, dark gaze from her, remaining hyper-focused on that area of her neck. It was then she felt the trickle of oozing moisture. Her skin stung like the very devil.

"I'm going to kill you," Declan told Rodrigo almost conversationally as he lifted his gaze from her wound. An unholy light glowed in his eyes and sent her heart into overdrive.

He meant it. If he could get his hands on the foolish Captain, he would rip him to shreds.

"Give it up, Rod," the rescue team leader snapped. "The man is unstable when it comes to his wife."

But Captain Oblivious was striving for mayhem, and his following words achieved it. "I can't. I've been in her bed, and she's a woman worth fighting for."

Declan's fierce expression froze before he pasted on a blank mask, and Claire died inside. He had to be thinking the worst of her. Yesterday she'd shown up with one guy, nearly had sex with *him*—her soon-to-be ex—and now a third was claiming to have slept with her.

"It's not true," she croaked. "Declan, I would never—"

"Be quiet, Claire."

His icy words were void of any feeling, and she fought back an onslaught of tears. God, she wished she'd never come to this cursed island. What wouldn't she give to turn back the clock!

CHAPTER 10

Claire assumed he believed Rodrigo.

Declan didn't.

The truth was that Captain Crackpot had them all beat in the built-body department, hands down. His physique put the SEALs to shame. But thank Christ, the overbearing baboon wasn't his wife's type.

For one, Rodrigo was too domineering.

Two, he refused to take her wants into account.

And three, she loved him—Declan.

Besides the quick glance when Thomas had first come aboard, and the one time she'd visually checked on Bonnie, she hadn't taken her eyes from him. She was looking to him to rescue her.

And he'd do it at the first opportunity. His legs were quivering and his quads were ready to call it a day, but Declan stood tall, waiting for an opening to pound the living hell out of the lying scum, Rodrigo.

He stepped closer and noted that the Captain straightened to his full height. That bastard had to be six-six if he was an inch. Rodrigo's massive frame was more than a wee bit intimidating, but Declan refused to show it.

Another step. Claire inhaled and held her breath.

Another step. The sound of a cocked gun behind him was chilling.

Another step brought him an arm's length from his objective.

"Stop right there, gimp. You don't want to be embarrassed before these lovely ladies, do you?"

Declan grinned, a smile more lethal in nature than cheerful. Rodrigo was in for a helluva surprise. His nemesis was unaware he'd taught Jiu-Jitsu twice a week prior to his accident. Declan only needed to get within striking distance. In the background, he heard Mac speaking with someone. His assumption was Alejandro, and it was confirmed when the ex-SEAL leader moved forward with a cell phone, which he held out to the obnoxious pirate.

"Alejandro needs to have a word with you."

The change in Captain Rodrigo's stance was immediate. He dropped the knife, shoved Claire into Declan's waiting arms, and strode off in the opposite direction, ripping off his billowing shirt as he went.

"Release my crew, Mac. Oh, and tell my cousin I'll call him tonight," he said as he climbed on the railing. "I apologize for the small nick, *mi tesoro*. It was purely accidental. One would never wish to hurt so lovely a woman. But hey, now you have something to remember our time together, yes?"

With a wink and a roguish grin, he swan-dived off the ship's side.

As exits went, his was splendid. Even Claire sighed in appreciation.

Reaching around her, Declan snapped his fingers once before her eyes. She came to and shifted to face him. Her wary expression hurt. Did she really think he had so little faith in her? Or did she have so little faith in him?

"So, you and Captain Clueless, huh?"

She snorted a laugh, lunging into his arms without further encouragement.

"He really was, Declan."

Closing his eyes, he held her tight. He'd lived a lifetime in the last fifteen hours.

"I can't believe this is on the fantasy menu," he said. "I think it took years off my life."

"Yes. Bonnie and I are going to have words," Claire promised.

"Not before Gavin bends her over his knee."

"Considering how happy she was to be abducted by pirates, I think Bonnie appreciates the kink."

Declan groaned. "Not something I care to know, sweetheart."

"Claire?"

Thomas approached the two of them and touched her arm.

Declan wished the guy would follow in Rodrigo's footsteps and take a flying leap into the ocean, but he doubted he'd be so lucky. Granted, he should be charitable toward Thomas for coming along on the rescue mission. While Thomas had done absolutely nothing, he *had* provided an extra body in case it was needed.

"Thomas." Claire smiled warmly and left the circle of Declan's arms.

He was suddenly bereft. Embarrassed at how he'd assumed it was him she wanted and not his rival, he limped toward his friends.

Gavin had pulled Bonnie to the side and was reading her the riot act.

"Ease up, Gav. She had no idea this would happen." Declan flared his eyes wide, giving her a warning glance. "Did you, Bon Bon?"

He almost laughed at how fast she picked up on his signal.

"N-no. Of course not," she stammered.

Declan hugged her. "You owe me," he murmured into her ear.

"I'm pretty sure I've already paid my debt. You don't know it yet," she replied in a low voice.

He pulled away to read her expression, hoping to get a hint. Her mischievous grin said she was referring to Claire. But why? His wife was safely ensconced in the arms of her new boyfriend.

Declan's gaze zeroed in on Claire across the expanse of the deck. She was holding hands with Thomas, and the two appeared deep in discussion, much too chummy for his peace of mind. Suddenly feeling old and tired, Declan staggered to the railing and studied the landscape.

The island was beautiful.

Admittedly, Captain Crazy had good taste in women and his headquarters locale.

For an insane moment, he wanted to take a page from Rodrigo's book. Wanted to fling off his shirt and dive into the aqua waters, never to return to real life. He judged the distance from the deck to the water. If he cut in at a clean angle, he might not break his damned neck. The only thing holding him back was leg-muscle fatigue. It would be downright humiliating if he needed to be rescued a few yards from the ship.

Giving up his foolish idea, he leaned heavily against the wooden rail. Soon, he would need to sit. But he'd take advantage of however many more minutes his legs would hold out first.

Mac approached to inform him that they intended to sail the ship back to Elysian Island. It would be more comfortable for everyone involved instead of riding back in the Zodiac.

"I need a place to rest so I'm out of the crew's way," Declan said softly, not wanting to make obvious his physical distress.

"Need an assist to the Captain's cabin?"

"No. I should be able to manage. Thanks, Mac."

Painfully, he straightened and worked his way toward the stairs. From the corner of his eye, he spotted Claire making haste to his side. He waved her away.

"Stay with your boyfriend."

He hadn't intended to be harsh, but walking required all his concentration. Her tight-lipped expression relayed exactly how she felt about his snarled words.

Fuck.

"Does someone other than me need to be castrated?" asked the frosty voice Claire had come to recognize as Bram's.

She appreciated his intervention because she wasn't sure how she would've responded to Declan's continual hot-and-cold routine. Could the accident have scrambled something in his brain, making him a moody shithead forever?

Either way, she was better off distancing herself from the situation. She loved him—her feelings would never change—but she'd be damned if she would take this ugliness day in and day out.

"No, he's doing that all on his own," she returned. "But I thank you for your offer."

She spun on her heel, ready to storm away.

"I can't believe she rejected Rod in favor of you," Bram's scathing tone rang clear across the deck.

"What the hell are you talking about?"

She half turned back. "Don't bother, Bram. He'll believe what he wants to."

If there was an emotional catch to her voice, well, it couldn't be helped. She was wrung out.

Sensing this, he gave her a little push toward his wife. "Go with Keira. Get some rest now."

She shocked everyone with the hug she gave him, but no one more than the first mate.

"Thank you," she whispered fiercely.

His back pat was awkward, as if he weren't used to such displays. He cleared his throat and once again shifted her to follow Keira. Pitching his voice low, he said, "She's a good listener."

Oddly enough, Bram was beginning to feel like the older brother she'd never had. Protective, gruff, and yet possessing a heart of gold. As she followed his petite wife to their cabin, Claire shut her brain off. No point in going over the day's events or Declan's bizarre behavior. She'd gain nothing by rehashing everything.

Upon entering their cabin, Claire gasped. Standing agog, she took in the opulent setting.

"This is your room?"

A chandelier hung from the ceiling, with what looked like real Waterford crystal. Claire knew quality when she saw it. She collected and sold rare finds via her web-based business. The bed was king-sized, with black and white damask bedding hosting deep amethyst accent pillows. Yards of the same purple material draped the headboard.

Along one wall, black bookcases held the classics and a variety of paperback romances from the 1970s to the present day. She immediately recognized the names of her favorite authors. A large silver tray with chocolate-covered strawberries sat on a massive table that took up a quarter of the room.

"This is my dream bedroom," she said on a sigh. "Can I be your sister-wife?"

Keira let out a hoarse bark of laughter.

"Seriously, I don't think I'd ever leave if I had someone who looked like your husband to bring me food." She met the other woman's sparkling gaze and grinned. "And here I thought you were being abused."

The smile disappeared from her new friend's face.

"I'm sorry. What…" she trailed off, unsure how to ask if she'd somehow misread the situation.

Keira put a hand to her throat and attempted to speak. The words came out in harsh croaks. "Was. Not Bram."

Tears burned behind Claire's eyes. She recognized that if this tiny, proud woman had not felt such a strong desire to defend her man, she wouldn't have spoken. Without needing to be told, she understood how difficult speaking was for Keira. Painful even. A very interesting story lurked in the woman's past.

"I'm sorry," Claire said again.

A calloused hand patted her silky soft one as a signal that

she was forgiven. Keira gestured to the bed and mouthed the word "rest."

"Thank you."

The second Claire's head hit the pillow, she was dead to the world.

CHAPTER 11

By midnight, they were back on Elysian Island, and Claire couldn't believe how long she'd slept onboard. Before she left the cabin, she wrote her information down so Keira could keep in touch if she chose. Claire hoped she would. They'd bonded with little to no words being spoken between them. Some friendships were like that, she acknowledged to herself as she hugged the other woman goodbye.

Declan was the first person she saw on the deck. A study of her surroundings showed that all other passengers and crew had gone. Focusing on him, she inhaled deeply and headed in his direction. There was no telling what would spike his temper, and she mentally prepared herself for another explosion.

As if sensing her presence, he turned in her direction. Moonlight shimmered off his blond hair. He wore it longer these days, and he blended with his current environment, looking a little pirate-like himself. The slight evening breeze rustled his locks, kicking up her desire to run her hand through his gorgeous, thick mane. It was one of the things she'd always loved when they had been together. Cuddling on the couch, or in bed, his head in her lap as her fingers stroked his hair.

God, she missed what they'd had. Seeing him again had dredged up bittersweet memories, along with all the past hurts. With a resigned sigh, she shut down her train of thought. None of it was important anymore. After today, she'd move on. Permanently.

Claire stopped a mere foot away, and they locked gazes but remained silent. It seemed each was loath to speak. Perhaps it was fear of another argument? A subtle shifting in his expression told her he was remorseful and about to apologize.

"Save it," she said, forestalling him. "I've heard it all before. Where's Thomas?"

His pained expression flashed, disrupting the calm composure. What had he expected? That she'd set herself up for another fall?

The earlier conversation with her now ex-boyfriend ended with apologies on both sides, but Declan didn't need to know the truth. Let him believe she was in the process of forming a meaningful relationship with someone else. Ultimately, it would be easier and allow her to save face.

"He went on when we docked about an hour ago. I guess he forgot you were going back with him," he said. She detected no malice, but he looked out over the beach, an inscrutable expression in place. "I waited to escort you back."

Her heart pinged.

A shuffling to her right had her peering into the darkness. A figure, all in black, lingered with one foot resting on the bulkhead he leaned against. The protective stance suggested it was Bram. Oddly, the man embodied a dangerous pirate more than Rodrigo did. With long, dark hair casually tied back with a strip of leather, the black billowing shirt, and the gold hoop in his ear, he appealed to her on a level the ridiculous Captain never had.

Lucky Keira.

Claire had only been half-joking about being a sister-wife.

"Your protector," Declan said, dryly. "He verbally flayed me alive earlier for being rude to you. Looks like you've earned yourself another champion, sweetheart."

Her heart hammered in her chest, and she refused to look at him when she asked, "Another?"

He reached out and tugged a lock of her messy hair. "You've always had me in your corner. I was lost for a while because of Jonah, but I'm back now, Claire-bear."

Her sinuses burned as tears flooded her eyes, blurring out everything before her.

"How can I be sure, Declan? These last two days have emphasized how volatile your temper is. You go from one extreme to the other. I refuse to live with that kind of uncertainty. I can't, and I won't."

"Jesus, I've done a number on you, haven't I?" He cupped her face, gently urging her to face him. "I love you, Claire. I always have, from the very first moment I saw you. I want to spend the rest of my life with you if you'll have me."

He paused and, when she didn't pull away, dropped a featherlight kiss on her lips and continued, "Between the emotional pain of losing our son and the physical pain from the accident, I..."

He shook his head and closed his eyes.

Still, she waited, not interrupting. His truth had been a long time coming, and he needed to open up, finally letting go of the heartache. His sobs started soft, eventually wracking his entire body. But she couldn't let him grieve alone. She wrapped herself around him, and they sat with their backs against the wood, sharing in the sorrow for the first time.

"I'm so sorry, Declan. I'm so sorry," she cried. "It was all my fault. If I hadn't insisted on picking him up—"

"No!" he denied, voice scratchy and raw. "No, sweetheart, it was never your fault. Not anything about that night was ever your fault. You never wanted to go out. *I'm* the one who talked you into it. I had a client to impress, remember?" He pressed his forehead to hers. "I said Jonah would get to his grandmother's and forget all about being sick. Your mother wanted us to stay overnight. Instead, I insisted on returning home. All I'd been thinking about was getting you to bed, our bed, and making love to you."

She choked back a sob at the memory.

"If anyone was at fault, it was *me*, Claire. *I'm* to blame for the circumstances leading up to the accident. My selfishness." He sucked in a breath and tightened his arms around her. "But the real reason he's gone is because some idiot, with an inability to use common sense and call a cab, drove under the influence. *He*"—Declan's voice broke—"*He's* the one to blame. *He* took our sweet boy. Not you. Never you."

The weight of self-hate lifted from her. His raw emotion and sincerity finally convinced her that he never held her accountable. All this time, she'd believed otherwise. Such a senseless tragedy had robbed her of a child, and the pain of that loss swept her husband away on a river of grief.

She buried her face against his throat and breathed in

the essence of him. God, his was a scent she missed. It smelled of home. Peace settled within her heart.

"I love you, Declan." His arms spasmed at her confession, but she continued, "More than anything or anyone, I love you. I didn't know how to go on after Jonah. After you'd spiraled down, there was no getting through to you. I didn't leave because I stopped caring. I left because I didn't know how to stop."

Declan's breath hitched in his chest. God, he'd waited so long to hear her say that. He'd been such a fool and nearly lost the only person who made him feel alive. Still, he had to know what was between her and Thomas.

"This isn't about jealousy, or maybe it is, but you and Thomas? Are you done?"

He felt her smile against his throat.

"We never started. Not really. This trip was to see if we were truly compatible," she said, snuggling closer. "He's a nice guy, and I feel terrible for dumping him after he came to the rescue, but he isn't you, Declan. He'll never be you."

Letting go of the breath he'd been holding, Declan kissed her. The need to taste, to confirm the truth, was too overpowering to resist, and he didn't give a shit if they had an audience with her menacing bodyguard. He wove his hands in her tangled mass of hair as his tongue skirted along hers, savoring the flavor of love. Kissing Claire was akin to coming home. He drank her in like a man dying of thirst. Long, mind-numbing minutes later, when things threatened to get out of hand, he forced himself to draw back.

"We need to find a cabin—pronto—or row ashore and

return to the cabana. Either way, we won't be coming up for air for a while."

Her happy laugh made his soul sing.

"Will you use pirate speak and have your wicked way with me?" she teased.

"Absolutely not! That fantasy is no longer allowed. It's to be banished forever," he growled, nipping at her lip.

"Oh, I don't know, I think you'd make an excellent pirate."

"Better than Captain Clueless?"

"Much," she laughed.

"What about tall, dark, and broody?"

"Bram? He's married, and Keira refused to allow me to be a sister-wife. She's a bit territorial," she deadpanned.

He mock scowled, or maybe he didn't. Declan didn't like the fact that she found the other pirate sexy.

"Yeah, all pirate fantasies are off the table," he declared firmly. "It's not open for negotiation."

"Hmm. I was looking forward to the motion of the ocean."

"Trust me, you'll get enough motion when we return to the resort. It might take you a while to get your land legs back."

She laughed as he intended her to. A smiling, happy Claire was a glorious thing.

Later, as Declan rowed them toward the shore, she questioned what he'd signed up for.

"I didn't."

"Everyone had to. It's part of booking at the Enchanted Tides Resort. Bonnie took care of the one for Thomas and me, though she never said what it was." She snorted. "We all discovered the hard way, didn't we?"

"Yeah, she was still apologizing to Gavin when he hauled her off the ship."

"Will he forgive her anytime soon for not making him the center of her fantasy?"

"I don't know. He was pretty livid at how underhanded the whole scheme was."

Declan sincerely hoped their friends didn't break up because of what essentially constituted a game on Bonnie's part.

"So you and Gavin never filled out the form? It was all Bonnie?"

"Yep. Apparently, she assumed we wanted to rescue our women."

"But if you *had* to choose something, what would it have been?" Claire asked, adorable in her curiosity.

He didn't pretend to think it over. "You," he said simply. "My fantasy has always been you, Claire."

She launched herself across the dinghy, nearly capsizing the small vessel. He caught her and shifted to steady the boat.

And in that moment, he realized he'd always catch her. As he always should've. Even when they were old and gray, he would be there for her. He never intended to let her down again.

"Sleep, shower, or sex?"

"Does it have to be just one? I'd kill for a shower," she said, stripping off her clothes.

Declan's mind went blank, and all he could do was stare as his wits abandoned him. He would've sworn he recalled every patch of skin clearly, but Claire in the flesh was much more beautiful than his memory in those long, lonely morning hours.

His hot eyes trailed along her back and ass as she made her way toward the bathroom. She paused and half-turned, glancing behind her with a sultry expression.

"You coming?"

"Probably faster than you'd like," he quipped and hurried after her.

Under the spray of water, Claire took her time soaping his body, her hands not missing an inch. Declan appreciated the hell out of the attention she spent on his lower half. Not just sexual in nature, but also the kneading of his over-worked leg and low back muscles. He almost wept with gratitude.

Then it was his turn to soap her. He took the opportunity to sit on the shower bench and urged her to stand before him. The fine stretch marks on her stomach reminded him of all they'd lost. His touch, reverent in nature, skimmed along those beautiful lines. She hated them, but for him, they were proof of their perfect son's existence.

Her sniffle brought his head up. Minus the previous night of aborted oral sex, this was the first time they'd touched each other in love since that fateful December evening. He knew well the emotions it evoked. He'd experienced them all and then some.

"Do you want more children?" he asked softly.

The question had been a constant in his mind. There was no replacing Jonah. But maybe they could fill the emptiness with love for one another and a baby or two.

"I do. But whenever I think about it, I feel like I'm betraying him."

He understood. The same thought had occurred to him. There was no easy way to escape the guilt. Children weren't interchangeable, and if he and Claire moved on, if they found happiness again, it seemed they weren't honoring Jonah's memory.

But it wasn't true. Their son would always hold a special place in their hearts.

Guiding her to straddle his hips, he said, "Let's make a baby."

Her tearful nod was all the answer he needed.

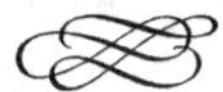

"No. I'm not going," Claire stated, shaking her head and backing away.

"Sweetheart, we've been through this. We can't not go. It just isn't an option," Declan said with a patience he didn't feel. Panic was building, making it difficult for him to inhale deeply.

She huffed out a breath and perched on the bed's edge. "No, Declan. I mean it."

Scrubbing his scalp in frustration, he looked to her mother, Julia, for help. All he received from her was a shrug.

A cry was wrung from Claire as the next contraction hit, and he almost lost his shit. At times like these, he pulled out his newest mantra, WWBD—what would Bram do?

Probably toss her over his shoulder and cart her stubborn ass to the hospital is what he'd do.

Not helpful.

"Bram!" he hollered over his shoulder. "Get in here!"

"You bellowed?" Bram's drollness didn't amuse Declan in the least.

"Yes. She listens to you. Talk some damned sense into her, will you? She can't have the twins at home." With that, Declan stormed from the room, grabbed his keys, and walked the overnight bag to the car.

As he slammed the trunk, he was surprised to find his hands shaking. Claire's fear was more than understandable. His own misgivings were suffocating him. Today was the third anniversary of the accident, and by mutual agreement, they'd decided never to go anywhere on New Year's Eve.

Unfortunately, they didn't have a choice this time. Their babies intended to be born early.

Declan double-checked that the car seats were secure. All he had left was to grab Claire's favorite snacks and get her into the delivery room without bloodshed. Preferably without *his* bloodshed. Her hormones were all over the place, and in the moments since her contractions started, he feared for his life.

A soft cry caught his attention, and he glanced up sharply. Bram was carrying Claire, with Keira and Julia trotting close behind. After settling her in the passenger seat and fastening the seatbelt, he stood and stretched, hands on his back.

Declan shot him a grin. "You're my hero, you know that?"

"You owe me. You can start by providing the name of a decent chiropractor in this godforsaken town." Bram pulled his soaked black designer sweater away from his skin. "And a competent dry cleaner. Your wife's water broke, and this is cashmere."

"Shit!" Jumping into action, Declan ran for the driver's seat. "See you at the hospital. Julia knows where it is."

"Text me when you arrive," Julia said, kissing his

unshaven cheek. She pitched her voice so only he could hear. "I don't need to tell you to drive safely."

"No, ma'am. You don't."

A quick hug, and they were off. They made it to the hospital with little time to spare. Apparently, their kids were eager to make an appearance. After a no-nonsense nurse whisked Claire away in preparation for her c-section, Declan left to find a parking spot. When he returned, he checked in and began pacing, waiting for a staff member to retrieve him for the procedure.

Gavin and Bonnie arrived shortly after Julia, Bram, and Keira.

"Looks like the old gang's back together," Gavin noted, hugging Keira and shaking hands with Bram. "I can't believe you'll be working with us."

The ex-pirate chuckled in the face of Gavin's continued disbelief that he'd been a marketing director for a Fortune 500 company. Declan found out Bram quit to follow his heart, aka Keira, when she fled to Elysian Island to recover her health. After a brief conversation with Gavin, they'd hired Bram as a temporary replacement so Declan could stay home and assist Claire with the twins. Depending on how well they all meshed together, they hoped to bring Bram on as a permanent partner.

"Someone has to take up the slack. Declan's going to be useless from lack of sleep," Bram said.

The group's mood was happy and light.

While Declan could appreciate their support, he experienced a strange detachment, separating him from their small crowd of family and friends. Today was one of the two days each year he let himself be moody-as-fuck because Jonah wasn't with them any longer. His son's birthday and the anniversary of his death were torturous, and rather than pretend, he allowed himself to grieve. Declan always made sure Claire was in a good place before isolating himself.

He'd promised himself never to let her down, and he meant it. Asshole Declan was gone forever.

"Mr. Braddock?" The delivery nurse tapped him on the shoulder to attract his attention. "Mr. Braddock, we're ready for you now."

He pasted on a smile, fooling no one, and followed the nurse.

"Declan." His wife held out a hand, and he gripped it like a lifeline. One would think *he* was scheduled for surgery, considering how nervous he was.

The doctor removed their daughter first, who squalled until her brother joined her.

Jesus! Twins!

No matter how prepared he and Claire believed they were, their babies would prove them wrong, just as Jonah had.

Their newborns were cleaned, weighed, and thoroughly checked over while Declan looked on. Then came the hospital IDs with the sensors. He assured Claire they had all their fingers and toes, as well as both ears, during the process. Her chance to hold them close after she was stitched up, bathed, and the last of the surgical trays was removed.

She promptly unwrapped each baby and counted their tiny digits for herself.

"Did you think I was lying to you?" he laughed.

"Shut up. It's a mother thing."

He leaned in and dropped a lingering kiss on her lips. "You're amazing. Thank you."

Their son's wide yawn caught their attention, and Claire started crying. Of course, it didn't take a genius to understand why. He was a spitting image of Jonah when he was born.

Declan tucked in next to her, careful not to bump his tiny daughter, and gathered Claire to his chest. "Let it out, sweetheart. It's okay. You're allowed to miss him."

The staff left them to their privacy.

Sometime later in the evening, after everyone had imparted their well wishes, snapped photos for posterity, and delivered gifts, they were alone again. None too soon as far as Declan was concerned. Claire couldn't keep her eyes open anymore, and he was worn to the bone, with his back aching like a bitch. Even still, exhaustion or no, his wife refused to release the twins into anyone else's care.

Declan gave in to her wishes and lined the bed with pillows so she could sleep holding them close.

As he kept watch, his thoughts turned again to Jonah. He'd have been dancing at the notion of becoming a big brother. Declan knew it on a cellular level. And now, in the silence of the wee hours of the morning, he imagined he heard his firstborn's giggle. Of its own volition, his hand drifted to the spot above his heart, and he pressed his palm flat to the wall of his chest. The ache would never truly go away.

Yet as he stood there, gazing down at a dozing Claire with a bundle tucked in the crook of each elbow, he had the stray thought that maybe, if the pain didn't leave, it was okay to embrace it. Perhaps Jonah was somewhere, jumping up and down with excitement.

Love filled Declan, providing the acceptance of the past he so desperately needed. Right now, at this very moment, he could move on and allow himself to embrace happiness again. With tears streaming down his face, he did what he couldn't do before. He bid a silent goodbye to his darling boy, shutting the book on that chapter of their lives. Jonah would never be forgotten, but the future and his family required his undivided attention.

IF YOU LOVED THIS BOOK, PLEASE LEAVE A REVIEW.

THE SEER, book 3 in the Sentinels of Magic series, is next to be released. It's the story of Fintan Sullivan, an Irish-born psychic whose fate is tied to the Aether's sister-in-law. He's loved her from afar for years, knowing she is destined to be his downfall.

Expected Release: May 2025

Following The Seer is *DISCOVERED MAGIC*, book 15 in The Thorne Witches® series. Wilder Thorne discovers the fiancée he believed perished in a climbing accident is still alive, and he's determined to do whatever it takes to bring her home. Even if that means traveling back in time to do it.

Expected Release: October 2025

ENDURING MAGIC

BOUNDLESS MAGIC

The Unlucky Charms Series:

PINTS & POTIONS

WHISKEY & WITCHES

BEER & BROOMSTICKS

COCKTAILS & CAULDRONS

WINE & WARLOCKS

HIGHBALLS & HEXES

The Sentinels of Magic Series:

THE AETHER

THE DEATH DEALER

THE SEER

THE TRAVELER

The Angels of Legend Series:

LUCIFER

CONTEMPORARY & ROMANTIC SUSPENSE

The Stonebrooke Series:

BURNING RESOLUTION

HIDDEN RESOLUTION

The Holt Family Series:

GOODBYE TO YOU

THIS TIME YOU

INCLUDING YOU

<u>*A LIFE WITH YOU*</u>

The Fiore Vineyard Series:
<u>*PICTURE THIS*</u>
<u>*RETURN HOME*</u>
<u>*ONE WISH*</u>

ABOUT THE AUTHOR

T.M. Cromer is a multi award-winning, bestselling author, who loves to craft wildly entertaining stories designed to keep you glued to your seat, turning the pages to find out what the hell happens next. She specializes in kickass heroines and the men who adore them.

Genres she writes include romantic fantasy, paranormal romance, and romantic suspense.

If you want to stay up to date on what's happening in the world of T.M. Cromer, please subscribe to her newsletter or text JOIN to 1-877-795-1526 to receive release news and promo alerts.

You can also join her VIP reader group on Facebook to chat with her, participate in polls, or keep current on what's happening. Become a member today!

FOLLOW T.M. CROMER:

facebook.com/tmcromer
instagram.com/tmcromer
tiktok.com/@tmcromer
pinterest.com/tmcromer
amazon.com/stores/T.M.-Cromer/author/B011QK3WXY

www.ingramcontent.com/pod-product-compliance
Lightning Source LLC
Chambersburg PA
CBHW071946190726
48293CB00004B/1382